3.9   570 Lexile

Shadow of a Doubt

s. l. rottman

Ω
PEACHTREE
ATLANTA

Also by S. L. Rottman

HERO
ROUGH WATERS
HEAD ABOVE WATER
STETSON

Published by
PEACHTREE PUBLISHERS, LTD.
1700 Chattahoochee Avenue
Atlanta, Georgia 30318-2112

www.peachtree-online.com

Text © 2003 by S. L. Rottman
Cover illustration © 2003 by Michelle Hinebrook

Cover design by Loraine M. Joyner
Book design by Melanie M. McMahon

Manufactured in the United States of America
10 9 8 7 6 5 4 3 2 1
First Edition

ISBN 1-56145-291-2

Library of Congress Cataloging-in-Publication Data

Rottman, S. L.
  Shadow of a doubt / written by S. L. Rottman.-- 1st ed.
    p. cm.
Summary: As his sophomore year in high school begins, fifteen-year-old Shadow joins the forensics team, makes new friends, and struggles to cope with the return of his older brother, who ran away seven years earlier and now faces a murder trial.
ISBN 1-56145-291-2
[1. Brothers--Fiction. 2. Family problems--Fiction. 3. Forensics (Public speaking)--Fiction. 4. High schools--Fiction. 5. Schools--Fiction. 6. Runaways--Fiction.] I. Title.
PZ7.R7534 Sh 2003
[Fic]--dc21   2003004790

*With heartfelt thanks to all my family,
but especially to my son Paul,
for taking enough naps to allow me to finish this book.*

❧

Special thanks goes to Carolyn Williamson,
for being a great forensics coach,
adviser, and GWHS Patriot.

And to my editor Vicky Holifield,
who has earned a week at a spa after all
the blood, sweat, and tears I put her through.

Chapter One

My fifteenth birthday marked the seventh year that Daniel had been gone. We didn't jump anymore every time the phone rang or someone knocked on our door. But there were times when the house got quiet, and I knew without asking what Mom and Dad were thinking about.

Even though I was a lot younger than my brother, we had been very close. He was my best friend. I guess he was my only friend. For nearly six months after Daniel left, I hadn't spoken to anyone, unless they spoke to me first. And then I only answered with one or two words. Mom took me to a psychologist after the first month of this behavior, but the shrink was convinced that I was mourning in my own way, and that I would get over it in time. He suggested my parents find a new activity to interest me.

They tried everything: model planes, drum lessons, even bird watching. Dad focused on sports, and I suffered through three days of karate, a week of swimming, two soccer practices, and almost two weeks of basketball before he finally gave up. Nothing worked. Without Daniel, nothing was interesting.

When I was ten, I found the library. We weren't supposed to be inside during recess, but the new librarian was a pushover for anyone who would sit quietly and read. I loved the peaceful and safe library much more than the chaotic noise of the playground. I

almost ate fantasy books. The idea of different worlds and crea-
tures fascinated me. Maybe I thought that in a different world
trust and love could remain unbroken.

My fifteenth birthday also marked my first year of high school;
I was finally a sophomore. I was eager to get to the new school.
Junior high had been boring and predictable. In high school, I
could pick some of my classes and get into subjects that actually
required thought. Plus, two other junior high schools fed into the
high school, so I'd be meeting new people. At Watson Junior
High, I had stayed pretty much to myself, but I hoped to change
and make new friends this year.

I showed up for high school registration dressed the way I normally did: black jeans and a black T-shirt. The new twist was the
black leather jacket I had purchased with my birthday money. I
had begun wearing nothing but black in the middle of the eighth
grade. I liked the way it worked with my dark hair to make me
look really pale. I was almost six-one, and the black accentuated
my scrawny height. I had overheard some people say I looked like
a vampire. I didn't really mind. I thought vampires were cool.

Dad had quit bugging me about the way I dressed, mostly
because he was convinced I was following a trend. Mom, however,
still hated it. A couple of weeks before school started, she bought
me three new brightly colored shirts, some blue jeans, and a pair
of khakis. She left a new outfit on my bed that first morning, hoping I'd wear it. She offered repeatedly to take the morning off and
go with me to registration, but I kept telling her I'd be fine.

Even though my parents didn't like the fact that I wore all
black, I knew they wouldn't do anything about it. They'd been like
that ever since Daniel left. They'd tell me what they wanted me to
do or not do, but they never told me I *had* to do anything. The
only thing that they really insisted on was that I always tell them
where I was going and when I would be home. If the plans
changed or if I would be late, I was expected to call. I never really

challenged their authority anyway. I sensed that it would be a terrible thing for all of us if I did.

Once, when I was ten, I was a few minutes late coming home from the library. When I got there, Mom was already on the phone with the police. She had called the library, and they had told her I wasn't there, so she'd panicked. For a long time after that, I had been afraid to be late. Now I figure being on time or calling if I'll be late is the better alternative to putting one or both of my parents in the hospital from a massive heart attack.

My fifteenth birthday wasn't any big party, but it was memorable for all of us. We were about to enter uncharted waters.

Daniel had been fifteen when he ran away.

A big banner above the door said, Palmer Panthers Welcome You! but the atmosphere at the school didn't seem overly friendly. I passed several tables where kids were signing up for clubs and activities. A bunch of cheerleaders in short skirts were selling T-shirts in one corner. I got in line in front of the registration table. The woman sitting behind it called "next," and I stepped up. Her neutral expression didn't change when I gave her my last name.

"Thompson...let's see. Oh yes, Thompson. Ernest—?"

"Shadow," I interrupted.

"Excuse me?"

"I go by Shadow."

She glanced down at my card and raised an eyebrow. She looked me up and down, studied the classes on my schedule, and began shaking her head. "Yes, well...um...Shadow, there appears to be a problem with your schedule. Step over to the line behind the next table, and they should be able to straighten it all out for you."

"What's wrong with my schedule?" I asked.

"They've put you in trigonometry and college prep chemistry."

I took my card and glanced at the rest of the classes. "My schedule's fine," I said. "Where do I go next?"

"Are you sure? You're—" She stopped and tried again. "We offer personal finance, auto shop, life science… That schedule is very…" She hesitated, as if she suddenly realized there wasn't a nice way to tell me it was a difficult schedule without making it obvious that she already thought I was an idiot.

"It's fine," I repeated. "Where do I go?"

She directed me over to the yearbook photographer. Although they assigned registration times alphabetically, everyone else seemed to have a group of friends to stand in line with. I saw a few people I recognized from Watson, but I didn't know any of their names, which was just as well. I wouldn't have known what to say to them anyway. I watched people watch me while I waited in line. I could tell the rest of the adults were forming the same opinion of me that the secretary had.

I'd been looking forward to a fresh start in high school, a chance to break out of the box I had put myself in. But it looked like nothing was going to change.

A guy wearing a black trench coat, combat boots, ragged jeans, and a Megadeath T-shirt came up and tapped me on the shoulder.

"Yo, you got a cigarette I could bum?"

"I don't smoke."

"Serious?" He seemed to be shocked. "Sorry, man." He turned around and walked off.

I sighed. Maybe someday I'd meet somebody who could actually wait until they knew me to form an opinion about me.

"Next," the photographer called, sounding incredibly bored.

I stepped up and sat on the little stool.

"Okay," he said, not looking up from the camera, "put your feet on the tape on the carpet, and turn your chin this way."

I complied.

"Good. Now take your sunglasses off."

Chapter One

"That's okay, I'll leave them on."

"I can't take your picture until you take your glasses off."

"Why?"

"Is there a problem here?" A very official-looking man dressed in a suit came up to see what was going on.

"I don't think so," I said.

The photographer made a face. "He won't take his sunglasses off."

"You have to take your sunglasses off," the man said.

"Why?" I asked again.

For a moment he seemed dumbfounded that I wasn't obeying immediately. "Because we don't allow students to take their pictures with their sunglasses on."

"Okay," I said, sliding off the stool, "Then I won't have my picture taken."

The man in the suit scowled. "You have to have your picture taken."

"Why? I'm not buying any."

"We need it for the yearbook."

I shrugged. "I probably won't buy one of those either," I said. I could tell the man in the suit was trying to control his anger.

"We need it for the school ID card."

"Fine," I said, getting on the stool again.

"Take your sunglasses off!" the photographer growled.

"Four people in front of me had their pictures taken with their glasses on."

"Those were corrective glasses, not decorative ones," the photographer said quickly.

"How do you know these aren't corrective?" I asked.

The man in the suit folded his arms across his chest. Without taking his eyes off me, he said, "Just take his picture."

Click. The camera flashed and I slid off the stool.

"Next," the photographer said in a relieved tone.

"Thanks," I said as I walked past him. "Now the rest of your day will seem easy!" He gave me an irritated look. I started toward the next line, the one to get my locker assignment.

"Just a moment." The man in the suit was still frowning.

"What?" I asked. I carefully kept my tone calm.

"What's your name?"

"Shadow."

"Shadow? Do you have a last name to go with that?"

"Thompson."

He stared at my face for a moment. "Daniel Thompson's brother?"

Embarrassed by the sudden tightening of my throat, I just nodded at him.

"Well, Shadow Thompson, my name is Mr. Barnett. I'm the Dean of Students. Do you know what the Dean of Students does?"

"You deal with discipline problems."

"Among other things, yes. So let me make this simple for you, Mr. Thompson. Classes start next week. If any teacher asks you to remove your sunglasses, or your leather jacket, or any other accessory you may have on, you will do so immediately. If you don't, you will begin the year serving detention for defiance. Is that clear?"

I nodded again.

"I have the feeling we'll be seeing a lot of each other this year," Mr. Barnett said.

"I doubt that'd be good for either of us," I muttered.

"What was that?" he said sharply.

Before repeating my remark, I took a good look at his face and decided that this was going the wrong way. "Nothing," I said. I went and stood in the next line.

"You are a dead man."

I turned around to find a short guy with big glasses and an even

6

bigger nose standing behind me. His head came only halfway up my chest. I had to laugh.

"Is that a threat?" I asked.

"Not from me. From Mr. Barnett. He picks a target and he won't forget it. Your next three years here are going to be hell."

"How do you know?"

"My brother. He graduated a couple of years ago. He had a run-in with Barnett his first year, and Barnett never forgave him."

I shrugged. "I don't plan on talking to Barnett any more," I said simply.

"Good luck," he snorted. "I've heard it's not always that easy." After a few seconds' pause, the little guy asked, "What's your name?"

"Shadow. Shadow Thompson."

"Good to meetcha, Shadow," he said, pushing his glasses further up on his nose. "I'm Vernon Thomas."

"Next." The lady didn't even look up to see if I had stepped forward or not. "Name?"

"Thompson."

"Ernest Thompson?" Before I could reply, she was holding a card out for me. "Locker number 815. Next. Name?"

Vernon hustled up and gave his name. I stood off a few feet, looking around to make sure I had done everything I needed to do.

"Locker number 814. Next. Name?"

Vernon looked over at me. "Looks like we're neighbors," he said, grinning.

"Yeah, it does."

He looked at his watch. "I've got fifteen minutes to kill."

"Waiting for a ride?"

"No. I saw a sign saying that there's a meeting for the forensics team at ten-thirty in room 28. I'm going to check it out."

"Forensics?"

"Yeah, you know, speech and stuff."

"You like speaking in front of people?" I asked. I had gotten Cs in English class every semester we had to give a speech. I did not enjoy speaking in front of large groups.

"Not a lot," he admitted. "My cousin did it a couple of years ago and said it was really cool. Plus, I like to argue. Debate is part of the forensics team."

I raised my eyebrows. "A team that lets you argue? That could be interesting."

Vernon tilted his head toward the hallway. "Want to come? It's open to everyone."

"I don't know. I'm not good with speeches."

"I bet you could argue if you gave it a try. You sure didn't back down for the photographer or Barnett."

I shrugged. "All right." I wasn't going to join the team, but I had nothing else to do. I wanted to try to make a few friends this year. This was a good place to start.

As we walked to room 28, we checked our schedules and found out that although we had most of the same classes and teachers, we had them at different hours. We did have chemistry together, and the same lunch period. We also discovered that he lived just two streets away from me.

"How come I never saw you at Watson?" I asked.

"I went to a private school."

"St. Mary's?" I asked. The big Catholic school was the only private school I knew of in the area.

"Yep." He let out a long gusty sigh. "I fought with my parents every night last semester, trying to convince them to let me come to Palmer this year. I'm here strictly on a trial basis." He lowered his voice, presumably in an imitation of his father. "One screw-up and you're off to St. Mary's so fast that your butt won't feel the road rash till it's sitting in a desk in Sister Catherine's classroom."

I laughed. "Guess you don't want to screw up."

Vernon laughed back. "Well, I certainly don't want to get caught!"

There weren't many people in room 28. In fact, there were only three.

"Is this the room for forensics?" Vernon asked.

The two guys with their heads bent over a Gameboy ignored us, but the girl in the corner nodded before returning her full attention to her book. The room had a dull feeling about it. The desks were in rows and there were only one or two posters on the walls.

"Well, we are a little early," Vernon whispered, trying not to show his disappointment.

I raised my eyebrows but sat down at a desk next to him anyway.

For the next five minutes, the room was silent except for the occasional beeps from the Gameboy. Six more people stuck their heads in the door to take a peek, but only two of them came in, scuttling nervously to desks in the front row. We were all scattered around the room. It was obvious that this was not a meeting for the social butterflies.

I consulted my schedule again and realized that this was going to be my English room. From behind my sunglasses, I looked around, trying to get a feel for the teacher.

"What are you doing?" Vernon whispered.

"Why are you whispering?" I asked.

He shrugged and shook his head.

"I'm just checking out the room. Looks like it belongs to a pretty traditional teacher."

"You never can tell," Vernon said. "Sometimes people surprise you."

"True," I agreed, feeling hypocritical. Being classified as a stoner or a troublemaker simply because I wore all black was a pet peeve of mine. I resolved to give my English teacher a chance.

After another ten minutes, I was ready to leave. But just as I started to get up, four more guys and a cheerleader walked in. Even if the first guy hadn't been carrying a stack of papers and the second one wearing a Palmer Wrestling shirt, I could have picked them out as upperclassmen. They walked with a swagger and assurance that no one else in the room had.

"Okay." The one wearing the Palmer Wrestling shirt clapped his hands loudly to get our attention. When he turned and faced the room, he discovered how unnecessary that was. "Seven? Only seven of you?" The disappointment was plain on his face.

"You're all here for forensics, right?" the cheerleader said.

One of the newcomers shook his head. "I thought this was for the chess club."

"Nope," she said. "Wrong room."

"Oh," he said. He gathered up his stuff and left.

"Great," Palmer Wrestling said. "Now we're down to six new recruits." He sighed and pointed to the clipboard and papers the other guy had set on the desk. "Sign up, leave your address and phone number, and take a flyer. We'll see you next Wednesday after school."

The guys with the Gameboy stood up immediately and started for the desk. The girl in the corner picked up a purple backpack with a hot-pink fanged smiley face on the front and stuffed her book into a side pocket.

"We waited just for a sheet of paper?" Vernon complained. "Can't you tell us what this is all about?"

Palmer Wrestling looked at him. "That's what the flyer is for," he said, his tone adding the unspoken "moron."

"Then why have a meeting?" I asked. "Why not just pass out the flyers at registration?"

"What is it you want to know?" the cheerleader asked, cutting off Wrestling's reply.

The two guys finished filling in the information, grabbed a

flyer, and left. The girl with the book stood and slung her backpack over her shoulder, listening intently. Another guy also stopped to hear what was going on.

"How often do we practice?" Vernon asked. "How long do we practice?"

"Come on, Tess, let's go," said Palmer Wrestling.

"Go ahead, Pat. I'll be there in a minute." Tess, the cheerleader, turned back to us, but Pat didn't leave. "You'll practice every Wednesday from three to four-thirty as a team," she said, "and on your own as often as you need to. Next year, if you're still serious about forensics, you can take the class as an elective, but for sophomores it's an after-school activity."

"Okay," said the girl with the purple backpack. "So what exactly are we practicing?"

"It depends on what you choose to compete in. You can do debate, either Cross Examination, which is with a partner, or Lincoln-Douglas, which is on your own. Or you can do different interpretive selections. There's original oratory, humor, drama, poetry, and extemporaneous."

"We compete? Even the beginners?" Vernon asked, sounding a little anxious. "When? How often?"

"About once a month," one of the other upperclassmen said. "On Saturdays usually, but sometimes there are weekend meets that go Friday and Saturday."

"But sophomores rarely get to compete," Pat said, "so you don't need to worry about it."

"Unless the team stays this small," Tess added. "We may end up using everyone."

"How do we decide what to compete in?" I asked.

"Look," Pat broke in, "all of that'll be figured out at practice, okay?"

I looked at him. "How are we supposed to know if we want to sign up for something when we don't know what it is?"

Tess laughed. "You guys should sign up. You've got the stubborn determination you need in debate, and you dig for information. Besides, if you don't like it, you can always quit." Her tone held a challenge.

Before we could say anything, the girl with the purple backpack spoke up again. "How many people do we speak in front of?"

"It depends on what's going on," Tess said. "Right before a meet, you might run through your presentation in front of the whole team during practice. Otherwise, you might only do it in front of one or two people at a time. At some of the meets, only the judge and a couple of parents are there to watch; at others you can have an audience of up to fifty people."

"Any other questions?" Pat made it plain the answer had better be no. We were wasting his time. After a moment of awkward silence, he snapped, "Then sign up if you want to. Otherwise, go home."

Vernon and I looked at each other. I didn't really plan on staying with the team, but Vernon seemed to be waiting for me.

I shrugged and walked to the desk. "I thought we were supposed to be talking and debating," I said, signing my name with a flourish. "Isn't that what forensics is all about?" I grinned at Tess. She smiled back.

"You could use that killer dimple in interpretive readings too," she said. "Maybe you'll have to do both."

I didn't answer. The dimple was the reason I never smiled in pictures. I hated it.

Pat was looking at my name on the list. "Shadow? What, were you named after a favorite family pet?"

"I hope you don't write your own speeches," I told him, "because you're not very original." And then I walked out the door. It had been a long time since a comment about my name had gotten to me—turning fifteen had me thinking about Daniel too much.

Chapter One

Vernon caught up with me a few minutes later, just as I was leaving the building. "Hey, man, wait up."

"Sorry," I said.

He laughed. "You've got guts. Standing up not only to Barnett, but also to some senior who thinks he's tough. That girl was right, though. You should be on the team. You're good with words."

"I hardly said anything!"

"Yeah, but what you said and how you said it!"

I looked at him and snorted. "The whole time all I could think was, please, God, don't let my voice crack now."

Vernon laughed again. "It sure didn't show."

I shook my head and kept walking.

"Where're you going?"

"Home."

He stopped. "My mom's picking me up in front of the school in about ten minutes. We could give you a ride home."

Again I shook my head. "Thanks, but I'd rather walk."

"You sure?" Vernon looked a little hurt.

"Yeah."

"Okay. See you next week, I guess."

"See ya."

I knew Vernon was probably thinking I was brushing him off. I didn't mean to come across that way, but I didn't know how to tell him that without sounding really corny. No matter how often I tried to make myself act like the people I saw around me, I just couldn't get it right. I had hoped things would be different at a new school. But maybe I was wrong. Maybe there was just something wrong with me.

I didn't have to be home for another hour. I decided to stop at the library on the way home to see if they had the new Robert Jordan book. Along the way, I thought about the forensics team. Forensics sounded like it could be interesting, and having an after-school activity might get Dad off my back about getting involved in sports. At six foot three, he had always been a basketball junkie. He couldn't understand why I didn't want to play, especially since I was already so tall.

I wasn't sure I could speak to an audience at all, though, even a small one. Plus, it seemed clear to me that there was at least one complete jerk on the team. Did I really want to deal with that?

But it would be something new. And I was pretty sure Vernon and I could be friends.

Besides, if I wanted to change, joining the forensics team was almost the biggest leap I could make.

As I walked into the library, I took my sunglasses off, tucking them in the pocket of my jacket next to the forensics flyer. It was nice and cool in the library, an important detail when you dress in all black.

I browsed in the general fiction section, looking for something to catch my interest. They didn't have the new Jordan book yet. I prefer fantasy usually, but I'll read almost anything except romance or westerns. A couple of years ago I got into sci-fi. The first time a Star Trek conference came to our town, I was so excited I went all by myself. I didn't make it an hour. It was too depressing to see those geeky older guys walking around by themselves; it was even more depressing to think that could be me in a few years.

I pulled three books off the shelves, and went looking for a study carrel to use. I like to read a few pages of a book before deciding to check it out.

As I walked around, I realized I wasn't going to get a carrel. I finally spotted a small table in the back. Only one person was sitting there, facing the other way. On the table I saw a purple backpack with a pink vampirish smiley face on the front.

"Hi," I said. "Mind if I join you?"

She looked up, startled, and then shrugged. "That's fine," she muttered as she went back to reading.

I picked up the first book and leafed through a few pages.

blink. "No, you couldn't be that slimy." Her eyes were still focused on her book, but they weren't moving across the page. "An actress? No, then you'd just take drama or be in the plays. What else? A TV anchor?" She was still trying to ignore me, but I thought her lips twitched with a suppressed smile. "Or maybe a lawyer? No, You don't look bloodthirsty enough to be a lawyer. Hmmm." I definitely saw a smile. "You know, this would be a lot easier if you would give me a clue."

"You're not supposed to be talking, remember?"

"Oh, yeah. Well, that's one of my faults, my poor memory. Do you think forensics can help with that?"

"I think you need more help than forensics or any other school activity can give you. I think you need professional help." She began to gather her stuff again.

"Okay, okay, I'm sorry. I'll be good this time."

"Too late," she said.

"Please!"

She took pity on me and smiled again. "I really do have to leave. See you next week."

"So you're definitely joining forensics?" I pressed.

"I'm definitely going to think about it." She took three steps from the table, but then stopped and looked back at me. "Will you be at practice next week?"

"Will you miss me if I'm not?"

She continued walking and said over her shoulder, "See you around—maybe."

"Bye!" I said as she walked away.

Yeah. I had to give forensics a try.

Chapter Two

My last days of summer vacation sped by. I was pleasantly surprised when Vernon called and suggested we go to a slasher movie the next Saturday. Of course, I had to tell my parents who Vernon was, where he lived, what his phone number was, where we were going, and when I'd be home before I could leave for the mall. I wasn't supposed to keep any part of my life from them, because they didn't want another surprise like Daniel had given them. I hated what he had done to us.

When we came out of the movie theater, I asked Vernon casually if he knew the other people who had been there to sign up for forensics.

He gave me a strange look. "No. If I had known any of them, I would have talked to them."

"No, I know you don't know any of them. I meant did you know who any of them are? Like their names or anything?"

"I don't think so. I might have seen that girl in the corner around somewhere before, but I'm not sure."

"Oh."

"Why?"

I shrugged. "Just wondering."

"Did you know any of them?"

I shook my head.

Vernon began to grin. "But I bet you want to get to know one of them."

"Whatever."

"It's that upperclassman, isn't it?"

"Who, the cheerleader?"

"Yeah!"

"You're crazy. And anyway, I'm pretty sure she has a boyfriend."

"How can you tell?"

"Look at her, Vernon. She's gorgeous. And smart. Of course she has a boyfriend."

"I knew it!" Vernon gloated.

"I'm not interested in her. She's probably dating that wrestling musclehead anyway."

"But you're going to join the forensics team, right?"

"Might as well," I said, trying to sound nonchalant.

Sunday night Mom, Dad, and I had hamburgers for dinner and then sat around the living room. The TV was on, but I was paying more attention to my book. The phone rang, and Dad got up to answer it. "Hello?... Yes, just a moment, please." He held the phone out to me, eyebrows raised in surprise. Getting two phone calls in a week was rare for me. I usually only got calls from relatives on my birthday.

"H-hello?" I winced. There went my voice, cracking again.

"Hey, Shadow. This is Vernon."

"Hey," I said. "What's up?"

"I was just calling to see how you're getting to school tomorrow."

"I was planning on walking. Why?"

"I couldn't decide if I should walk or ride the bus."

"Well, if you decide to walk, meet me in front of the Mini-Mart at 7:15." Even though it meant a twenty-minute walk, I wanted to avoid the bus.

"Cool," Vernon said. "I'll be there."

"See you tomorrow."

"Bye!"

I hung up the phone and went back to my chair.

Mom and Dad were watching me expectantly. I picked up my book.

"Shadow?" Mom said in a prompting tone.

"What?"

"Who was that?"

I sighed but explained as quickly as I could. "Vernon. He's the guy I met at registration, remember?"

"The one who you went to the movies with?" Mom clarified. "Didn't you say you met him during the speech meeting?"

"The what?" Dad stared at me in shock.

"He's joining the speech club," Mom said smugly.

"I'm just thinking about it, Mom—"

"That's…different," Dad interrupted.

"Shhh!" Mom said. "Don't discourage him!"

"But what about basketball, or soccer?"

I ignored him. We had had that discussion a hundred times.

"What were you and Vernon talking about?" Mom asked me.

"We're going to meet before school tomorrow and walk together."

"Would you like a ride?"

"No thanks."

Before she could ask any more questions, I escaped to my room. I glared at the empty room down the hall. Because Daniel had shut our parents out, they had always forced themselves in on me.

The first day proved that high school would be as boring as junior high. It was a bigger building with more kids in it, but the teachers still acted like they expected most of their students to be idiots.

Chapter Two

I made sure I had a good book with me at all times.

Most teachers gave us alphabetically assigned seats. I liked that because it often put me in the back of the classroom. I ended up sitting behind Vernon in chemistry. We were also assigned as lab partners for the entire year.

I looked, but I never saw Robin. She wasn't in any of my classes, and I didn't see her during passing periods, either. I hoped she had been serious about joining forensics. I was getting impatient for Wednesday's practice.

After school on Tuesday, Vernon invited me to his house to work on our first trig assignment. We had the class at different hours, but so far the teacher was giving the same pages for homework. I called Mom as soon as I got there, and then I stayed for almost an hour. The last three problems stumped us. We promised to call each other later when we figured them out.

I hadn't been home for ten minutes before the phone rang.

"I've got it!" I called, and picked up the phone. "H-hello?" My voice cracked again.

"You know, you've really got to fix that," Vernon said.

"Yeah, yeah, yeah," I said.

"Well, I've got number 23."

"Really? Cool." He walked me through it. Once he told me the step we had missed, it came together quickly. "Thanks, man."

"No big deal. But now *you* have to do number 24."

"I'll call you when I get it," I promised.

I sat down at my desk and started to work through the next problem.

"Shadow, dinner's almost ready!" Mom called.

"Be there in a minute," I hollered back.

The phone rang again. I couldn't believe Vernon had figured out number 24 so fast!

"Hello?" Thankfully my voice didn't crack this time.

"Shadow?"

"Yeah?" I didn't recognize the voice at all.

"Shadow, it's Dan."

"Dan who?" I asked.

It was quiet for a moment and then the voice said, "Daniel. Your brother, Daniel. I just…just… Look, I'm sorry… Tell Mom and Dad I'm sorry, okay? That's all I wanted to say… You still there, Shadow? Shad?"

I'm pretty sure that's when the whole world came to a stop. A low buzzing started in my ears.

"Shadow? You still there?"

My stomach began launch preparations.

"Man, don't hang up!"

I dropped the phone and backed away from it like it was radioactive. I tripped over my chair, knocking it to the floor with a loud crash. Mom came running to my room.

"Shadow? What's wrong?"

I couldn't say anything, couldn't take my eyes off the phone.

My mother's face was full of concern. "Shadow, are you okay?"

I shook my head, still staring at the phone. After what had just happened, I wouldn't have been surprised if it had flown away. Daniel's voice started squeaking through it and I flinched.

With a puzzled look, Mom picked up the receiver while still watching me. "Hello?" she said cautiously.

Slowly she raised her hand to her mouth. Her eyes welled up with tears. I had never seen anyone's face actually glow before, but at that moment, hers did.

Daniel must have been talking a mile a minute, because she didn't say anything. Finally she simply said, "Oh, Daniel!" and started crying.

I closed my eyes and opened them again. I was still on the floor, and Mom was still on the phone. Apparently it had really happened. Daniel had called. How often I had wished he would come back home! But instead of being happy, I felt strangely empty.

Chapter Two

"Mark!" Mom screamed down the hall suddenly, making me jump. "What?" she said into the phone. "Why?... Where are you?" The joy in her face seemed to drain away. "You're where?... Why? What happ—?" Then she shook her head. "Never mind, never mind. You can tell us when we get there."

"Get where?" Dad asked from the door.

"Of course we're coming!" Mom said into the phone. "We'll be right there!"

"Where?" Dad asked again.

"I love you," Mom whispered into the receiver. "We'll see you soon." She hung up the phone gently, reluctantly.

It was quiet. Dad and I were staring at Mom, but she didn't take her eyes off the phone.

Suddenly I felt weird sitting on the floor. As I struggled to get up, Dad crossed my room quickly and reached down a hand to pull me up.

"You okay?" he asked, helping right the chair.

"Yeah."

"You sure?"

I nodded.

We both looked at Mom expectantly. Finally, Dad said, "Caroline? Mind telling me what's going on?"

His voice seemed to break the spell. She clapped her hands like a little girl. "Come on! We have to go!"

"Go? What's going on?"

"Daniel! Daniel's come back to us!" She was disappearing down the hall.

"Daniel?" Dad hurried after her. Their voices became indistinct murmurs in their bedroom.

In a daze, I walked into the living room and sank into the couch. Daniel was coming home. So many times, I had imagined the moment. But now that it was real, I didn't know how I felt. I tried to organize my thoughts, but they stayed jumbled in my head.

Where had he been all this time? What did he look like now? How long would he stay? He was twenty-two years old now—he couldn't be planning on staying here forever. Why hadn't he called before? Why was he calling now? What did he want?

Mom and Dad rushed through the living room and out the door to the garage, without ever glancing in my direction. I wasn't really surprised they had forgotten about me. After all, this was the moment they had been waiting for, ever since that horrible morning when my brother had disappeared.

"Shadow!" Dad bellowed, opening the door. "Hurry up!"

I slouched a little further into the cushions, wishing they really had forgotten me.

"Shadow!" he called again, striding back into the house. He was halfway across the living room before he spotted me, drawn as tightly into the couch cushions as I could get.

"Come on! We haven't got all day."

"No," I said. My voice sounded strange to me. "We've got years. That's how long he left us to wait."

My father's face became very stern. "I'll pretend you didn't say that. Now let's get moving. Visiting hours end soon."

"Visiting hours?" I felt my stomach clenching up, preparing for a blow. How many times had I imagined him hurt or sick or starving and all alone? How many times had I cried, thinking he must already be dead? "Is he in the hospital?" I asked weakly.

"No," Dad said curtly. "He's in jail."

I had thought there couldn't be any more surprises; I was wrong. "Why? What did he do?" I asked.

"We don't know. He didn't have time to explain everything to Mom."

"He didn't have time? Or he didn't want to because he was afraid you wouldn't come see him?"

Dad's face turned a little pink. "Let's go. We don't have time for this," he said, heading back to the door.

Chapter Two

I still don't know if I didn't move because I couldn't or because I didn't want to.

He opened the door to the garage, barely pausing to ask, "Are you coming?" before slamming it shut behind him.

I listened to the car doors shut, and a few seconds later, the garage door. The house was silent except for the ticking of the clock. About ten minutes after they left, the phone rang. I let the machine answer. It was Vernon, bragging that not only had he been the first to solve number 23, he had also now solved 24 and 25. If I wanted the answers I was to leave $25,000 in unmarked bills in his mailbox and call him back. Just as everything got quiet again, the oven timer buzzed loudly. I tried to ignore it, but it got on my nerves. I finally got up and turned off the timer and the oven. The ticking clock seemed to get even louder in the silence. It was strange, because it felt like the world should have stopped. But it kept on going.

What did my brother want from us now? That was the thought I couldn't get out of my head.

What did he expect from us?

What could we expect of him?

I walked slowly down the hall, past my room into Daniel's. Without turning on the light, I stretched out on his old bed. Daniel had gone on a rampage the night before he left. Mom had insisted on putting everything back into place and leaving all his stuff in his room. She washed the sheets and comforter every month, and they smelled fresh. For years, I had sneaked into his room, imagining the day he would return, or sometimes even pretending that he had never run away. I knew his room by heart.

Even without looking, I knew the names of the bands on every poster on the wall. The stereo and speakers were back in place, and the CDs he hadn't destroyed or taken with him that night were arranged in a rack. I knew Daniel's skateboard was still propped against the wall inside his closet. His clothes were hanging neatly on the rod, a lot neater than he had ever hung them. I had never understood about the clothes. After a couple of years, my mother had to know that they wouldn't fit him even if he did return.

My parents had always talked about *when* Daniel would come home. I don't know when that phrase had changed in my mind, but it had never changed for my parents. I had talked about when Daniel would come home for a long time, but eventually it had become *if* Daniel would come home, and finally I had quit talking about it altogether.

My parents' *when* had become *now.* And I didn't know how to feel about it.

Chapter Three

When I heard my parents come in, I was still lying on Daniel's bed. I blinked in surprise at my watch. It was nearly 11:30 P.M. I must've fallen sound asleep.

I heard their muted voices in the kitchen. Getting up crossed my mind, but I didn't have the strength. After a few minutes, the hall light clicked on. A triangle of light spilled into the room, just touching the corner of the bed.

I heard footsteps heading into my parents' room across the hall. Someone else walked to my room, paused in front, then came to Daniel's door and pushed it open. The sudden light was blinding, even with my arm over my face.

"Aaah!" I blinked hard a few times, trying to adjust to the light before I lowered my arm to see who was there.

My father was leaning against the door frame. "Your mother is very upset," he said.

"Why?" I asked. "What did Daniel do?"

Dad shook his head. "She's upset with you!"

"With me? What'd I do?"

"You made us lie to Daniel. We had to tell him you were too sick to come see him."

"You didn't have to lie to him."

"We didn't want him thinking his only brother didn't want to see him after seven years."

I snapped my mouth shut so hard my teeth hurt. Staring at the ceiling, I focused on keeping my teeth together. Silence was better than anything I might say to him. Daniel left us—never even called for seven years—and only decides he needs us after he gets arrested. But my parents were mad at *me* for not throwing my brother a welcome party.

"You were gone a long time."

"You know it takes a couple of hours to get to Denver," he said calmly.

"Denver? Is that where he's been all this time?"

"Yes."

Denver. So close and yet so far. Our local station and newspaper sometimes carried Denver info, but only big stuff.

"Talk to me, Shadow," Dad said, trying to sound encouraging. "What's going on?"

"Why did he call?" I blurted out.

"Because he missed us."

"Now? After seven years? It took seven years for him to miss us?"

"He's missed us for a long time. It took seven years to get the courage to call us again."

"I don't get it. What's he want?"

Dad hesitated. "He wants to come home."

"No, what does he *want?*" I insisted. "He must want something from us, or he wouldn't have called all of a sudden."

"He wants our family—" Dad began.

"But why *now?* What is it about now? Why not four years ago? Last year? Ten years from now? What's so special about now?"

"Shadow, we have to give him a chance," Dad tried again.

"What's he in jail for?" I demanded. "What did he do?"

"He's not really in jail. He's just being held until the arraignment. They'll do that tomorrow, and decide if they've got enough to hold him over for trial."

"How long have they been holding him?"

"He's been in custody for a few days now."

"Are you going to pay the bail for him?"

Dad nodded.

"What did he do?" I asked again.

"We don't think— He didn't do anything. He's accused of…" Dad's voice trailed off.

"Accused of what?"

Forcing the word out, Dad was barely able to say it loud enough for me to hear. "Murder."

My brain refused to process the word. My brother, who used to give me piggyback rides and always gave me half of his candy bars, was sitting in a jail cell.

While I was silent, Dad hurried on. "It can't be true. There's no way our Daniel could have killed someone. He was just in the wrong place at the wrong time. He's innocent."

"So that's why he calls now," I muttered. "He needs bail money." Then I asked, "What makes you so sure he didn't do it?"

"Shadow!"

"Well, what makes you so sure?" I repeated. "He hasn't been 'our' Daniel for a long time. You say a trial date's going to be set and they're releasing him on bond, so somebody thinks he did it! How many other times has he been arrested?"

"This is his first arrest," Dad began, but I was on a roll.

"How do you know he hasn't killed lots of people? How do you know he hasn't been arrested before and there just wasn't enough evidence to convict him? Maybe someone on the jury just had a shadow of a doubt." I read John Grisham and watched *Law and Order;* I knew what I was talking about.

Dad's face tensed up and he took half a step toward me. "This is Daniel we're talking about," he ground out, his voice shaking. "He's your brother!"

I was quiet, staring at the comforter. I was ashamed of what I had said, but I wasn't going to take it back. Just because it was an uncomfortable thought didn't mean it was impossible.

I could feel Dad's eyes on me. Long seconds dragged out. Finally he sighed. "It's late."

"I know."

He hesitated for a minute, like he wanted to say something more, but then he turned and walked away. I stayed on Daniel's bed a little longer, and then I went to my room and closed the door. I never turned on any of the lights.

When I woke up, I was still on top of the covers, fully dressed. Sunshine was streaming in my window. I sat bolt upright and looked at the clock. Almost 9:00!

Frantic, I rushed to the bathroom, tore off my clothes, and hopped into the shower. I finished in record time, wrapped the towel around me, and stepped into the hall.

Through their doorway I could see Mom and Dad sitting on the far side of their bed. They were talking quietly. It looked like they were arguing about something. I racked my brain. I was positive it was only Wednesday. What were they doing home?

Dad looked around. "It's about time you woke up. Another ten minutes and I was coming in to get you."

I walked a little closer.

"Don't you think you should apologize to your mother for last night?"

I chewed on my bottom lip for a minute, and then very carefully said, "I'm sorry you had a rough day yesterday, Mom."

She acknowledged my apology with a slight bow of her head. She was pale and tight-lipped. Dad glared at me.

"What's going on?" I asked in confusion. "Why aren't you guys at work?"

"We're bringing Daniel home today," Mom said simply.

Chapter Three

I stared at her for a moment, waiting for more, but apparently she thought that explained everything.

"Why didn't you wake me up? I'm late for school."

"Daniel's coming home," Mom repeated. "You're not going to school. Now, get dressed. We've got a lot to do."

"Mom, I need to go to school. I've got three assignments due and forensics practice after school."

Dad shook his head. "You can turn the assignments in later."

"This is the first forensics meeting. I *have* to be there."

"You can go next week. I'm sure your friend will tell you about whatever you miss today."

"You don't understand," I said. "I don't want to miss school today."

"Shadow, I think your brother is a little more important than some club meeting," Mom said, sounding exasperated.

"It's the first meeting of the year!" I protested. When they didn't say anything, I exploded. "It's not fair! He messed everything up when he left! Why does he get to screw it up all over again?"

"Shadow!" Dad said sharply.

I went back to my room, trying not to stomp. I quickly got dressed and put my books into my backpack. Grabbing my jacket, I headed for the kitchen.

"Shadow!" Mom called from her room. "You and your father are going to get Daniel's room ready, while I run out to the store. I don't know if Daniel's going to want to go out to dinner tonight or stay home, so I want to be prepared."

I grabbed some breakfast bars from the pantry and slipped out the back door, closing it quietly.

I walked down our street quickly, nearly jogging. I kept expecting to hear one of them yelling at me. When I finally turned the corner, I took a deep breath and slowed down. A little.

At school, the halls were quiet. Third hour had already started. I thought about trying to go to Dr. Anderson's class without a pass, then dismissed the idea. He was too structured and by the book. He would insist on a pass.

Sighing, I switched directions and headed toward the attendance office. It just happened to be right next to Mr. Barnett's office.

I gave the secretary my name and explained that I needed a late pass.

"Is it excused?"

"I overslept," I said.

She raised her eyebrows. "Into third hour?"

I didn't say anything, just nodded.

"We don't consider oversleeping an excuse," she said primly. "I'll write the unexcused pass, and you'll have to arrange detention with your first and second period teachers." She began to write me a pass. Right then, the door behind her opened and a kid kind of slouched his way out of Mr. Barnett's office. Mr. Barnett followed him.

"Ms. Day," he said to the secretary, "Mr. Spencer needs to sign up for in-school suspension for the remainder of the week." The kid sat in one of the chairs against the wall.

Ms. Day finished writing my pass and started to hand it to me.

Mr. Barnett intercepted the pass. "Mr. Thompson? Why are you late?"

I hesitated, and Ms. Day answered for me. "He claims he overslept."

"I didn't *claim* to oversleep. I really did oversleep!" I suddenly realized I wasn't using the best tone. "I forgot to set my alarm last night," I added quietly. Mr. Barnett gave me a fatherly smile—the kind of smile my father gives me when he knows he's caught me doing something wrong.

"Why don't we step into my office, Mr. Thompson?" he said, gesturing toward his door.

I sighed and tried not to roll my eyes as I walked into his office and stood in front of his desk. He shut the door and sat down in his chair. "You almost broke your brother's record," he said mildly.

"What?"

"He got detention on the first day of school," he said. "Why are you late, Mr. Thompson?" He gestured for me to sit down.

"Shadow."

"What?"

"I'd rather be called Shadow."

"I'm calling you Mr. Thompson to show you respect."

"Yeah, right," I mumbled. "It sounds more like you're patronizing me."

"That's not my intent."

"Please call me Shadow. If it will make you feel better, I'll even call you Arthur." His nameplate was sitting front and center on his desk, facing me.

"No need to get smart with me, young man."

"Why do adults always say that when a kid makes a point?" I asked.

Mr. Barnett actually smiled. A begrudging smile, but a smile. "Okay, Shadow, I get your point."

"Thank you, Mr. Barnett," I said, doing my best to keep the sarcasm out of my voice.

"Now, can we get back to our problem?"

"I overslept. It won't happen again." Then I added, "I don't think."

"You didn't just decide to cut class?"

"No. In fact, I have my trig homework from second hour and I'd like to go turn it in."

"If I call home, is there someone who could back you up?"

"Please don't do that," I said a little too quickly.

"Why not, Shadow?" Mr. Barnett asked innocently. "Would that get you into trouble? Were you someplace you shouldn't have been?"

"No, but I am now," I muttered.

"Excuse me?"

I slumped a little further down in the chair. "I got in a fight with my parents this morning," I began reluctantly.

There was a sudden knock at the door.

"Yes," Mr. Barnett snapped.

The door opened partway. Ms. Day smiled apologetically. "Mr. Barnett, I'm sorry to interrupt, but Mrs. Thompson is on line three right now, and she sounds a little agitated."

"Thank you, Ms. Day." The door closed softly. Mr. Barnett watched me thoughtfully for a moment before picking up the receiver. "Mrs. Thompson, this is Mr. Barnett, Dean of Students. How may I help you?... I see.... Yes.... Yes, he is here.... Uh-huh.... Okay, I'll be sure that he gets the message.... Certainly.... Thank you." He hung up the phone and considered me carefully before beginning. "Your mother said you left the house without permission to come to school this morning." He sounded a little confused.

I nodded, staring fixedly at his nameplate.

"She asked me to tell you that you're to come straight home after school today."

I grimaced.

"That bothers you?"

"I have forensics practice after school today."

"Would you like to call her back and let her know that?"

"She knows," I said bitterly.

"Would you like to tell me what's going on?"

I shook my head.

Mr. Barnett waited another minute, but when I didn't say anything else, he scribbled on my pass and then handed it to me. "You'd better get on to class," he said. His eyes almost looked sympathetic.

I stood up and took the pass from him. When I reached the door, he said, "Mr. Thompson...um...Shadow?"

Chapter Three

I turned to go.

"If you need to talk, my door is open."

"Thanks," I said, and then left as quickly as I could.

On my way to class, I looked at the pass. He had changed it from an unexcused to an excused tardy.

"So where were you this morning?" Vernon asked as we were leaving chemistry.

I shook my head. "Long story. Long, boring, ugly story."

Vernon grinned. "Sounds like the kind I should ask about."

"I wish you wouldn't."

"Okay," Vernon said, shrugging agreeably.

We went to our lockers, and then split up again to go to different classes, planning to meet back at our lockers before lunch.

As I made my way through the crowded hallway, I collided with someone and several books fell to the floor.

"Hey, watch where you're going!" an angry voice exclaimed.

"Sorry," I muttered, stooping down to retrieve the books. I glanced up and then smiled. It was the cheerleader from the forensics meeting.

I stood and handed her the books.

"Slow down a little in the hallways," she advised. "It doesn't look cool to hurry. And it's really uncool to bump into people."

"Sorry," I said again. "Will you be at practice today?"

"Of course," she said, flashing me a grin. "I'm one of the co-captains, so I have to be there."

I stared after her for a second, admiring the way her denim skirt swung from side to side, then hurried to class. In spite of her advice to slow down, I didn't want to get an unexcused tardy. One trip to Mr. Barrett's office was enough for the day.

During class, I had a hard time concentrating. I kept trying to force Daniel from my mind, but I wasn't having much luck. I couldn't believe the way my parents were jumping up and down about my brother coming home, acting as if there wasn't anything wrong, going on as if he hadn't been accused of—I couldn't finish the thought.

He'd left us seven years ago, shattering our family. I still found it almost impossible to trust people or get close to anyone. I was always afraid of doing something wrong and driving them away. And now, just when my life was beginning to get normal, Daniel comes parading back home, disrupting everything again.

Even if he hadn't come home, it seemed as if his reputation at school was going to be a problem for me. Mr. Barnett wasn't the only teacher who remembered Daniel. My English teacher actually seemed to turn a little pale when I admitted I was Daniel's brother. I wondered exactly how much trouble my brother had gotten into in the short time he was a student here.

It really bugged me that my parents wanted me to rearrange my schedule around Daniel, as if he hadn't rearranged my whole life by leaving. How could my parents just take him back with open arms and no questions? How could they expect me to do the same thing?

I tried to think about the cheerleader, but that just made me wonder whether I should go to forensics practice, and that led me straight back to Daniel. Part of me was dying to see him. What did he look like now? I had so many questions about how he had managed to survive for seven years on his own. I wanted to know why he left, and why he came back. Part of me couldn't wait to see him. But another part of me didn't want to see him at all.

Of course, I would have to see him. There was no way to avoid that. So under what circumstance did I want to meet him? Did I want him coming into the house with me there, waiting for him? Or did I want to come home after he was already there, showing him that he wasn't the most important person in my life anymore? Should I go straight home after school because my parents had told me to? Or should I disobey them and stay for practice, knowing that they would worry when I wasn't home on time?

All these thoughts tore through my mind like a tornado, ripping away the calm security that I had struggled to find for the last few years. When the bell rang, it felt like class had only lasted five minutes. And I had no idea what had happened. I wasn't entirely sure if the substitute had been male or female.

"So what do we do in civics?" Vernon asked at our lockers.

"I have no clue."

"What do you mean? Weren't you just there?"

"Sort of." I shook my head, shoved my books in my locker, and slammed it shut.

In the lunch line, Vernon tried to get a conversation started, but after a few monosyllabic answers from me, he fell quiet too.

We paid for our lunches, and then wandered over to the table we had been sitting at for the last two days.

As I picked up the piece of cardboard that passed for pizza in the school cafeteria, I felt bad that I had brushed Vernon off. I asked him if he had any brothers or sisters.

"Yeah," he said, "an older brother and younger sister. How about you?"

"I don't know," I said. About four years ago I had started telling people I didn't have any brothers or sisters; it was easier than explaining everything.

"You don't know?" Vernon laughed, but it was an uncomfortable laugh. "You don't know if you have brothers or sisters? You don't know what you did in the class you were just in? What are you, strung out on-crack or something?"

I shook my head and put my half-finished pizza on the plate, shoving the tray away from me. "No, but I'm wondering if that might help me." I put my head down on the cafeteria table.

"Shadow, what's going on?"

Lifting my head, I stared past him through the windows. "I had a brother. When I was eight, he ran away. We never heard from him again. Until last night."

Vernon's eyes got huge. "He's still alive?"

I nodded.

"And he just showed up last night?"

"No, he called us. He's coming home today."

"When?"

"I don't know."

Vernon gave me a funny look. "Your brother's coming home today and your parents made you come to school?"

Shaking my head, I began ripping a napkin to pieces. "My brother's coming home and my parents told me *not* to come to school. They wanted me to stay there and help get a party together for him."

Vernon was quiet for a few moments, and I could tell he was trying to figure out what was going on. "Why don't you want to be there?"

"I don't know." I laughed bitterly. "My answer for the day."

"Well, I guess that explains why you're acting so weird. I fight with my brother all the time, and sometimes I say I wish he didn't exist, but...I...I can't imagine my life without him."

"That's how I used to feel—well, the part about not imagining a life without him. Now, though, I can't imagine a life with him back."

"What happened when he ran away?" Vernon asked.

Vernon really seemed to care. He wasn't just interested in the gossip. For the first time in years, I told the story.

It was just a few days after my eighth birthday, and the most important thing in my world was my big brother. I wore his hand-me-down clothes, played with his old toys, and followed him around so much that I wanted everyone to call me Shadow, just like he did.

Chapter Three

But it seemed like Daniel had been changing, since about the time I turned seven. He and my parents fought all the time, although I didn't always understand what they were fighting about. Sometimes it was about his new friends, sometimes it was about his curfew or his grades, and sometimes about the clothes he wore. And my parents fought with each other about what to do with him.

That summer, he wouldn't let me be his shadow anymore, and got mad at me when I tried to follow after him anyway. He started sneaking around. And I'd sneak around too, trying to be like him. Since I couldn't go where he went, I'd wait for him at the end of our street. Then I'd walk home with him, pretending we had been together the whole time.

One night, Mom and Dad were both in the living room, just sitting there. They were waiting for us. I got a funny feeling in my stomach.

Mom came over to me. "Shadow, what time were you supposed to be home?"

"Five-thirty," I said softly.

"What time is it now?"

I looked at my new watch, a silver one just like Dad's that I had been given for my birthday. "Almost seven."

"Shadow, you're old enough to tell time, and you're more than old enough to follow the rules. I want you to go to your room and think about this. You're restricted to your room for the rest of the night."

Slowly I turned and shuffled toward my bedroom. From the hallway, I was able to hear almost everything my parents and Daniel said.

"What's the problem?" Daniel asked.

"What's the problem?" my dad repeated in disbelief. "You have so many problems, I hardly know where to begin!"

"Mark—" Mom started.

"But the first problem is your attitude," Dad continued.

"Too bad," Daniel said, and I could picture his shrug.

"For you!" my dad countered. "Your attitude has got to change, and so does your total disregard for our rules."

"How about your attitude? How about your need to be in control of everyone? It drives you crazy that I'm an adult now and you can't tell me what to do anymore."

"One, you're not an adult yet—"

"Bullsh—"

"Two," Dad raised his voice to cut Daniel off, "I can tell you what to do. I'm your father and you're living under my roof. And three—"

"You're such an asshole! I can't even—"

"Watch your language!" Dad yelled.

"Please," Mom said, "Please let's just sit down and—"

"I'm outta here," Daniel said.

"That's it!" Dad shouted. I heard him jump up from the couch. It sounded like he threw the table across the room. "I will NOT tolerate your defiance any longer! You—"

It was at this point that I decided I would be better off in my room, so neither Daniel nor my parents would catch me eavesdropping.

I'm not sure how long I lay on my bed, curled up with the stuffed tiger Daniel had given me for my fourth birthday. Eventually the shouting stopped and the house got quiet. At one point, Mom knocked softly on my door and brought in two peanut butter and jelly sandwiches and a large glass of milk. She told me good night and ruffled my hair before giving me a kiss on the cheek.

A few moments later, I heard her knocking on Daniel's door.

"Go away!" he shouted. "I have nothing to say to you!"

"I thought you'd like—"

"I don't want anything from you!" he yelled. For a while I

could hear him throwing things around.

After that, it was quiet, almost too quiet. There wasn't a sound coming from Daniel's room, not even his stereo or TV. I sat on the floor by my door, holding my tiger, and hoping Daniel would come talk to me the way he used to. Finally, barely able to keep my eyes open, I got up, stripped down to my underwear, and crawled into my bed.

In the middle of the night, I woke up. I thought Daniel was in my room, but when I sat up, no one was there. I decided I must have been dreaming.

When I went into the kitchen the next morning, Mom asked me to go tell Daniel we were having pancakes for breakfast.

I knocked timidly on his door, and then a little louder. "Daniel? It's me," I said, knocking again. When there was no answer, I carefully and quietly turned the knob and opened the door.

The window was open and the drapes were fluttering a little, letting in bits of light. Daniel's room was always a mess, but now it looked like it had been destroyed. Torn papers and posters were everywhere, books and CDs were scattered all over, and the desk chair was lying on its side in the middle of the room.

But Daniel's bed was neatly made, with a piece of paper lying in the center of it.

I took a couple of steps into the room, toward the bed, looking around. "Daniel?" I whispered again, frightened. Only the curtains flapped in answer.

I looked at the paper. There were just three words, in large block letters:

I HATE YOU

I turned and ran out of the room, hollering, "Daniel! Daniel is gone!"

When Daniel didn't come home the next day, the police were called, the school was notified, all of Daniel's friends were questioned. No one knew where he was.

Every time the phone or doorbell rang, we all jumped. Mom and Dad practically raced to answer it, hoping for news. As the days passed, however, we became less hopeful, and more fearful of what the news might be. Weeks went by, and we still asked each other if anyone had seen Daniel.

"I still remember all of us sitting quietly around the dinner table three months later, on Daniel's sixteenth birthday, wondering where he was and if we would ever see him again. And it turns out that we will get to see him again," I finished. "We just had to wait seven years."

"So that's where you got your nickname," Vernon muttered.

"What?"

Vernon kind of shook his head. "I didn't want to ask so I just kind of assumed that you took the name Shadow 'cause, you know, it's better than Ernest."

I got up and threw my lunch away. When I returned, Vernon was kind of toying with his empty milk carton. "You going to practice today?" he asked, pushing his glasses up on his nose.

"I haven't decided yet."

"I know it's none of my business, and you haven't asked, but I think you should skip practice. I'll tell you everything that happens. Go home and see your brother."

Chapter Four

Cautiously I opened the front door, actually afraid of what I might see. I couldn't begin to imagine what Daniel looked like now. Would he look like Mom? Or Dad? And the fact that he had been in prison was setting my imagination on fire. Would he have long, scraggly hair, or would he have shaved it all off to look tough? How many scars would he have on his face? After all, I was pretty sure that all accused murderers must have at least one scar.

I peeked around the door, not stepping immediately into the house. All was quiet. The living room drapes were drawn and there were no lights on. The house had an empty feeling to it. Sighing, I went inside and headed for the kitchen. I wanted to grab some food and then get to my room as quickly as I could.

"What was that sigh for?"

I probably jumped a foot straight into the air. As I landed, I kind of crouched, ready to ward off blows.

"Jeez, Shadow, you're jumpier than a cat!"

I took my sunglasses off, but in the dim light I could barely make out the person sitting in the armchair by the fireplace. I straightened up.

"I didn't think anyone was home."

"I noticed," he replied. "Mom and Dad went to pick you up. Apparently they missed you."

Neither of us said anything for several moments that felt more like years. I didn't move. I didn't want to go into the living room, because then I didn't know how I'd escape later. Questions kept flying through my mind, but I rejected them quickly. They all sounded accusing, even to me.

"I don't think I would have recognized you on the street," he finally said. "Looks like you got Dad's height."

"Almost," I said.

"Give it another year. I bet you catch him."

I had nothing to say to that. Daniel was sitting down and I had no idea how tall he was. As my eyes adjusted, though, I could tell that Daniel was stockier than Dad and I were, and his hair was short, but not shaved. His haircut looked almost trendy. He had dark hair like me and Mom, but he had Dad's strong chin. In fact, the way he was relaxing there in khaki pants and a rugby shirt, I would have never guessed he had just come from jail.

"I guess school just started. You a freshman now?"

"Sophomore."

"Watch out for the dean. I can't remember his name, but he is one big jackass."

"You mean Barnett?" I asked.

"Yeah, that's the dude," Daniel agreed.

"He's only a jackass to troublemakers and delinquents." *You know*, I added in my mind, *the kind that get arrested later in life.*

Before Daniel had a chance to respond, the door to the garage slammed, and Mom and Dad came rushing into the house. "Oh, good, Shadow, you're home," Mom said. She barely looked at me as she hurried over to Daniel.

Dad, however, did look at me. Sternly. "We don't appreciate what you did this morning. We'll talk about it later."

"...made reservations, just in case," Mom was saying to Daniel. She reached out and patted an imaginary stray hair back in place.

Chapter Four

"It's entirely up to you. We can go out to dinner, or we can stay here and have steaks."

Daniel shifted uncomfortably in his chair, leaning away from Mom a little bit. "Either way is fine. I don't care."

I started to walk down the hall toward my room.

"Shadow, what do you want to do?" Daniel asked.

"They didn't ask me." I stepped into my room and shut the door behind me.

It didn't stay shut long. I had just put my backpack on my desk chair when the door swung open again.

"Young man, I don't know what your problem is, but you had better get over it right now!" Dad hissed.

"What?" I exclaimed. "I just came in here to drop off my books and take off my shoes."

Disbelief was plain on Dad's face, but all he said was, "Come back into the living room, and bring an adjusted attitude."

Which attitude? I wondered. *The one where I fawn over Daniel for killing someone? Or the one where I thank my brother for ruining our lives without a second thought?*

"I'd rather stay here," I said.

"Then you'd better be ready to stay here for a long time," he said, glowering at me.

"Fine! Just tell Daniel I'm sick again. I'm sure he'll believe it now."

"Shadow," Mom said gently. Dad and I both jumped. Neither of us had seen her in the hall behind him. "Please. Your father and I just want to have our whole family back, okay? We want our family." Her voice quavered just a little. "Could you please try? I don't know why it's so hard for you, but could you just try for us?"

I couldn't remember my mother ever begging me for anything. "Okay," I said, shrugging uncomfortably. "I'll try."

Her eyes shone across the room. "Thank you, honey." She turned and disappeared down the hall.

I went back to my bag and began pulling my books out, stacking them on my desk.

As Dad started out of my room, he said, "You know, this isn't easy for any of us."

I raised my head slightly, but didn't say anything. It didn't seem to be all that hard for Daniel, and I didn't see Mom or Dad being really bothered either.

"Don't take too long," Dad added.

I didn't rush, but I didn't take as long as I could have, either. After I unpacked my books, hung my coat on the back of my door, and ran a comb through my hair, I took a deep breath and went back to the unknown.

In the living room, I walked into silence. Mom seemed eager to break it. "Daniel would like to stay home for dinner tonight, where we'll all be more comfortable."

"Good," I said, thinking that if this was supposed to be comfortable, I would rather die than go out where it would be *un*comfortable.

"Mom, I've told you I go by Dan now," my brother said, a little sharply.

"Oh, yes, yes," Mom said. "I'm sorry, honey. I'll really try to remember."

"You'll have to give us a little time," Dad said, "to get used to all the changes, Dan."

I decided not to sit down. "I think I'll get a soda," I said. "Does anyone else want something to drink?"

"I'd like an iced tea, please," Mom said, smiling at me.

"Got any beer?"

My parents both stared at Daniel for a minute, not answering right away. Daniel had only been fifteen when he left, but now he was twenty-two. Mom spoke up slowly. "I...I think there are a couple of light beers stuck in the back of the fridge," she said to Dad. "From the last office party we had."

Daniel wrinkled his nose slightly, but nodded. "I'll take one."

"Let me help you, Shadow," Dad said, getting up quickly.

He followed me into the kitchen with a tight face. I took four glasses out of the cabinet, then put one back and got a beer mug instead. Dad just stood there in front of the fridge.

After a couple of seconds, I said, "Dad? If you don't want to help, could you at least get out of the way?"

He flinched a little, and then opened the refrigerator. He handed me the pitcher of iced tea and a can of soda. He bent down, muttering to himself.

"What do you want?" I asked. He didn't answer right away, but then he stood up with two beer cans in his hand.

I raised my eyebrows but didn't say anything as I put one of the glasses back and got another mug. My parents occasionally had a glass of wine with dinner, but that was about it. We used the beer mugs mostly for root beer floats.

Back out in the living room, Dad handed Daniel his beer, and then lifted his mug for a toast. "To our family. May it stay whole for a long time to come."

Mom clinked her glass against mine. She turned to Daniel, but he was already drinking. She clinked Dad's glass and looked over at Daniel again. "Well, if we want to eat tonight," she said, "I'd better start getting dinner ready."

I stood up quickly. "I'll help."

"Oh, no, really, that's okay," Mom said, gesturing toward my chair. "Keep Daniel—Dan—company."

That was the last thing I wanted to do. But I had promised to try, so I sat back down.

It was quiet for a while. Even Dad seemed a little unsure about what to talk about. Daniel was staring into his mug, so I took the opportunity to study his face.

The haircut made him look preppy, but something about his eyes made him look…hard. He was frowning, and the lines on his forehead reminded me of Dad. I peeked at Dad; the lines on his face only made him look tired. When I looked back at my brother I noticed that he *did* have a scar—one on his left cheek, just under the eye.

"What'd you do to your face?" I asked, trying to sound casual. I was trying to think of what could have caused the scar. It was too small for a knife wound. Maybe he had gotten into a fight with someone wearing a ring or something.

"What?" Daniel sounded defensive.

"The scar." I pointed to my own cheek. "What'd you do?"

"I tried to pull a little brother out of a cactus bed when I was eleven. I've got a couple more on my neck and arms, if you want to see them."

"Oh," I said. "No, that's okay."

"You look good, Dan," Dad said. "Staying pretty fit."

Dan shrugged. "Small meals and needing to move fast was good for me, I guess."

"Moving fast?" Dad repeated blankly.

Dan made a dismissive gesture. "Nothin'."

"So did you have roommates?" Dad tried again.

"Yeah."

Dad waited for more, but Daniel apparently thought that was answer enough. "So…" Dad cleared his throat. "Um, Dan, what kind of job do you think you're going to get?"

Daniel looked up from his beer. "You mean if I don't go to the joint?"

Dad winced, but pushed on. "I just wondered what kind of work you were interested in."

"Don't know," Daniel said, shifting in his chair. "Hard to get a job without a diploma." He nodded toward me. "Remember that. Stay in school till you get one."

I felt like I was in a bad ad for public education.

"Surely you've had jobs," Dad pressed. "You must have some idea of what you want to do."

"I've done all kinds of jobs at one time or another. Didn't ever like any of 'em enough to stick with it."

"Like what?"

"Sales, services, errand boy, bookkeeper, entertainer, all sorts. Never stayed with any of 'em very long."

Dad was quiet for a moment, then chose what would seem to be the safest job to discuss. "What kind of sales? Furniture? Clothing? Did you work in a mall or a department store?"

Daniel snorted. "Not quite."

"So what did you sell?" I asked.

He looked at me out of the corner of his eye. "Nothing you'd be interested in."

"Where have you been?" I continued. "Where were you staying all that time?"

"I'd rather not talk about it right now." His voice had a sharp edge to it.

"Okay," I said slowly. He didn't want to talk about his future; he didn't want to talk about his past. I didn't know what to make of this stranger who was supposed to be my brother. "Did you really kill someone?" I blurted out.

"Shadow!" Dad exploded, sitting straight up in his chair. "That's enough!"

"It's okay," Daniel said, shaking his head. He turned cold eyes toward me.

I tried to meet that icy stare, but I couldn't. It was my turn to study my drink. Fortunately, Mom came bustling back in. "Okay, the steaks are seasoned, and the scalloped potatoes are in the oven. Whenever you're ready, you can start the grill," she said to Dad.

"I'll do that right now," he said, jumping up from his chair.

Envious, I watched him leave the room. Mom pulled a chair over closer to Daniel. "What did I miss?"

Daniel and I glanced at each other before looking away and simultaneously saying, "Nothing." For a moment, it was almost like old times—in the interest of self-defense, we both wanted to keep our problem to ourselves.

"Well, Dan, so much has changed," Mom said. "I don't even know what kind of food you like or anything. You'll have to give me a list of things you like, so we can get them for you."

"Don't worry about it. I probably won't be staying long."

I could have killed him for saying that. Mom looked like he had just knocked the wind out of her.

"Why not?" I demanded.

He smiled bitterly at me. "My trial will be coming up soon."

The hairs on the back of my neck rose. If he didn't think he'd be back after the trial…he must have done it.

Mom floundered, at a loss for words, but finally she patted his arm and said, "Honey, we're going to meet with a good lawyer tomorrow. Don't give up."

"The public defender told me the best I could hope for is ten to fifteen years for voluntary manslaughter."

"He didn't care about your case. He's swamped and looking for an easy way out. We're going to get you the best lawyer and—"

Dan shifted away from her. "Don't waste your money," he said.

I felt sick. It was hard enough to have him home again; I couldn't think of him going to jail. I stood up, trying not to wobble. "I'll go set the table," I said. I passed Dad as he came back into the living room.

I put out four plates, remembering back to the first year that Daniel had been gone. Mom had made me set four places at the table month after month, just in case my brother came home in time for dinner. The day Dad quietly told me that I only had to set it for three, Mom had spent an hour locked in her bedroom. When she came out, her face was puffy and her eyes were bloodshot. That was the last time I had seen her cry.

The timer went off. "Got it!" I called. I turned the buzzer and the oven off, but left the potatoes in to keep warm. Dad went out to the grill to flip the steaks. On his way back through the kitchen he managed a strained smile.

I glanced into the living room. Daniel had picked up a small statue off the fireplace. I wondered if he was pricing it. Suddenly I flashed back to the night Daniel had left and I had "dreamed" he was in my room. Two weeks later, when I was unable to find my piggy bank anywhere in my room, I realized that I hadn't been dreaming. I lost not only my hero that night, I had lost my Playstation savings as well.

Clearly I needed to settle down before I went back in there. I put the salad on the table and got out three types of dressing. Mom had set out a loaf of French bread on the counter. I sliced it slowly and put it in a basket. Desperately, I looked around the kitchen again, but couldn't find anything else to do. I went back to the living room.

Daniel was still standing by the fireplace. "The house looks good," he was saying. "Not much has changed. I thought maybe you'd be in a bigger house by now."

"No," Mom said quickly. "We're very happy with this house, and we love our neighbors. Besides, it's the perfect size for us."

I looked at Dad, but he was staring off through the window. My parents didn't disagree often, but they had fought several times over the last few years about moving. Dad did want a bigger house, at least one with a three-car garage, but Mom refused to even consider it. If we moved, she had always asked, how would Daniel be able to find us?

"How much longer for the steaks, Dad?"

"Hmm?" He blinked, then looked at his watch. "Oh, they should be ready any minute. We could probably move to the dining room."

"Any more beer, Shadow?" Daniel asked.

"I'm afraid those were the last two, son," Dad said.

So that was the reason Dad had taken a beer.

"We'll get some, the kind you like," Mom said. "We just don't drink much around here."

"There's Coke, Diet Pepsi, and 7 UP," I told him.

"I'll take a Coke," he said.

I almost offered to show him where he could find them himself, for future reference, but I firmly reminded myself I had promised Mom to try. Instead, I took the empty beer mug from him and went to the kitchen to get his Coke. I needed another one anyway.

By the time I had poured the two glasses, Dad was back in with the steaks, and Mom and Daniel were sitting at the table.

At least while we were eating we didn't have to talk. There was the minimal pass-the-salt and the-potatoes-are-really-good conversation, and that was about it. The quiet was almost a relief.

But then Daniel asked about our cousin Bruce, and that led to questions about other family members. In a few minutes they were having a great time, reminiscing. Old events, so old that I couldn't remember them, were brought back to life. Mom, Dad, and Daniel were talking over each other and laughing. It was just like the time Dad had an old college buddy over to dinner. I felt like an extra in a movie scene. I listened and put one forkful of food into my mouth after another.

When I finished my dinner, I stood up to clear my place.

"We've got apple pie for dessert," Mom said.

"I used to dream about your homemade apple pie," Daniel said.

Chapter Four

"I'm full," I said, even though I had only had one helping of everything. "And I've got a lot of homework tonight."

"You get good grades, Shad?" Daniel asked.

I shrugged.

Mom smiled. "You can do better than that, Shadow." She turned to Daniel. "He's been on the honor roll for the last three years."

"Very good," Daniel said, doing a golf-clap. I couldn't tell if he was mocking me or not. "What sports do you play, other than basketball?"

As I opened my mouth, Dad answered for me. "He doesn't."

"Just sticking with basketball, huh?"

"No, he doesn't do any sports, not even basketball."

"Really?" Daniel seemed surprised. "So what do you do?"

"Hang out mostly," I said before Mom and Dad got a chance to say anything. "Read a lot, surf the Internet, just do stuff."

"He's thinking about the Speech and Debate team this year," Mom added.

Daniel's eyebrows rose. "That's...uh...different."

"That's exactly what I said!" Dad exclaimed, gathering dishes from the table.

I glared at them both and then took my plate into the kitchen. Dad was right behind me.

As I left the kitchen, he said, "Shadow, try to hurry with your homework tonight, okay? Don't just stay in there reading. Come back out and join us."

I couldn't decide if he was ordering me to do it, or if he was asking because he wanted a little help with conversation.

My trig assignment took the most time, because I hadn't been in class to start it. I also had short assignments in chemistry and American lit. After I was done, I sat at my desk, staring at my library book. I had no idea what to make of Daniel. I wondered if he was just using my parents for the bond money. Would he skip town again and leave them with a huge debt to go with the shattered hopes?

I really didn't want to go back out to the living room. Daniel was the shining star tonight. I wondered how long his "guest" status would last. Would my parents ever treat him as their son again, as someone they could be honest with and voice their disapproval to? I had a sinking feeling that the time for that was long since past. Daniel had been gone too long to ever really be a family member; he would always be treated as a guest in our house.

With a sigh, I forced myself to get up from my desk and walk down the hall. It wasn't as quiet in the living room this time, because the TV was on. Everyone was looking at it, but I had the strange feeling no one was really paying any attention to the sitcom on the screen.

"Everything done?" Dad asked as I walked into the room.

"Yep."

"There's a piece of apple pie waiting in the oven for you, Shadow," Mom said.

"Thanks. I'll get it later."

Daniel glanced at me. "So, you still go by Shadow. When I started calling you that, I never thought it'd stick."

I did my best to keep my voice even. "Just because you left didn't mean everything about my life had to change. I liked the name Shadow. I still do."

"You look like one now, all in black like that."

"Thanks," I said, flashing a huge fake smile at him. I wasn't going to let him know he upset me. I wasn't going to let him control my feelings anymore.

I stood up without realizing I was going to move. Once I did, I had to go somewhere, so I headed for the kitchen.

"Hey, Shadow, catch me another Coke, would ya?"

"Right," I muttered. "Anybody else?"

Chapter Four

Mom and Dad said no.

From the kitchen I heard Daniel ask Dad, "Ya got any rum? It might make the Coke go down easier."

It was Mom who answered. "Yes, I think we have some rum. Don't we, honey?"

"I can fix a drink for you," Dad said in a tense voice. I could hear him rummaging around in the dining room cabinets.

I was pulling the pie out of the oven when Dad came in and got the Coke from the refrigerator. "Want another one, Shadow?"

"Does mine come with rum?" I asked, trying to joke. Bad timing. Dad gave me an unreadable look.

"I'll take milk," I said quickly. "It goes better with pie."

Dad poured the rum into the Coke, shaking his head the whole time.

"What's wrong?" I asked.

"Nothing," he replied curtly. A lie if I ever heard one.

Daniel had the remote and was flipping through channels when we got back. Dad handed him his drink and he took it without saying anything. Dad's mouth tightened in a thin line, but he was quiet as he returned to the couch.

"This is a good show," I said, when Daniel paused for a moment on channel four.

He waited a few seconds, then grunted, "Nah," and kept moving through the channels.

I turned my attention to my pie, resolving to finish it and then go to bed.

The phone rang, and I hoped fervently that it would be Vernon, calling to tell me about the afternoon's meeting. Mom picked up the phone, and in a few short words she told the telemarketer that he was interrupting a very important evening. She slammed down the receiver. I had never seen my mother come that close to being rude before.

A few more bites finished the pie. After I put the plate in the dishwasher, I stopped between the living room and hallway.

"Well, good night," I said.

"You're going to bed already?" Daniel asked.

"Yeah," I said, yawning as big as I could. "I had a long day. Besides," I added with a sidelong look at my parents, "I'm still fighting that cold."

"Just a minute, Shadow," Mom said, turning to Dad. "We need to decide what's happening tomorrow."

"What do you mean?" he asked.

"I can't take tomorrow off," she said. "Someone should stay home with Daniel."

"Not me!" I said instantly. "I'm not old enough to baby-sit him."

"I don't need anyone to stay home with me," Daniel said. "As long as there's a car I can use."

"No," Dad said before Mom could open her mouth. "I'm afraid that won't be possible." He gave Mom a meaningful look, which she chose to ignore.

"I could probably get a ride with Sonia," she said, "and you could use my car."

"Caroline," Dad said in a hard voice. "I said he can't use our cars."

Mom and Dad locked in a stare-down. Mom was clearly upset. I knew Dad was angry, but he looked calm.

"Hey, no big deal," Daniel said, shrugging it off. "I'll find a way to get wherever I need to go."

"I think it would be best if you stayed in the house," Dad said, not taking his eyes off Mom.

"You're not trying to ground me again, are you?" Daniel's tone was almost light.

Dad smiled, but there wasn't any humor in it. "Merely making a suggestion. You don't have money to buy gas anyway."

Mom turned back to me. "Are you sure you can't stay home tomorrow?"

Stubbornly, I shook my head.

Daniel laughed. "I think he's afraid of me."

"No," I shot back. "I just have better things to do."

"Boys," Dad said, refereeing just like he had when we were younger.

Mom ignored the whole side play. "Then I want you to come straight home after school," she said.

"I'll try."

"You'll try?"

"Yeah." I got defensive. "I missed practice today. I've got to find out what's going on. I might need to stay after a little bit."

"I'm sure it can wait till next week," Mom said firmly. "Come straight home."

I rolled my eyes. "Good night," I said again, escaping the room before I could be given another command.

I went to bed, but I stayed up reading. Dimly I was aware of Daniel and my parents coming down the hall and saying good night to each other. The house was quiet, and it was my favorite time to read. The book drew me in, and before I realized it, I had read the last hundred pages.

With a sigh and a stretch, I put the book down and blinked at the clock. Just after one. I yawned and decided to go to the bathroom.

When I opened my door, I was surprised to see a light coming from under my parents' door. They were never up this late.

Quietly, I walked to the door. I could hear murmuring, but couldn't make out any of the words. Just as I was about to knock and ask if something was wrong, the voices got a little louder.

"Caroline, I meant what I said!"

"We can't just leave him with a public defender!"

"I didn't say that! I said we can't afford Maclean! The bail alone set our investments back almost ten years! And Maclean's the most expensive lawyer in town!"

"Because he's good! Doesn't Daniel deserve the best?"

"Yes, but Bryce is a very busy—"

"You don't think he could work the son of his tennis partner into his schedule?"

"Of course, but—" Dad was almost shouting.

"Shhh! Do you want the boys to hear?" she asked.

Their voices became an indistinct murmur again. I returned to my room. I wondered how long Daniel—and their fights—would remain under our roof.

Chapter Five

The next morning when I went into the kitchen, I was surprised to find Mom there, already dressed for work and talking on the phone. She usually didn't get ready until after Dad and I left. "Thanks, Sonia, I really appreciate it.... Okay, see you in twenty minutes."

She hung up the phone. "Good morning, Shadow." She smiled, but she looked pretty frazzled.

"Morning. What was that all about?"

"Oh, Sonia's going to come pick me up today."

"Something wrong with the car?"

"No. But your father and I discussed it some more last night, and we decided to let Danny—Dan! I've got to get that right!—to let Dan borrow the car today."

"You and Dad both decided that?"

She was writing a note, so it took her a moment to answer. "Well, it makes more sense. If we can get an appointment today, I would have to leave work, drive home to pick him up, and then take him back downtown. This way Dan won't have to wait on me. He can just drive the car to the lawyer's office himself."

I nodded, even though it sounded weak to me. "Where's Dad?"

"He had to go in early to see about getting an appointment

with Mr. Maclean." Mom put the note in the center of the countertop. "Now, I've got to go finish getting ready. Don't forget to come
straight home this afternoon."

"I'll try," I said.

"Do better than try, Shadow. Be here." As an afterthought, she
added, "Have a good day."

"You too," I muttered.

I glanced at the note. It was for Daniel, of course. It said that
Dad would call later with the appointment time and that we
would be having dinner at 6:30.

I grabbed my breakfast bars and headed out for school. Vernon
was waiting for me at the corner.

"Two more minutes and I would have left without you," he
said in greeting. "I wasn't sure I wanted to wait as long as I did
yesterday."

"Fair enough," I said.

"So?" he said as we turned down the street. "How'd it go last
night?"

"It was…" *How was last night?* I shook my head. "I don't know."

Vernon laughed. "Sounds like you're in the same condition you
were in yesterday."

"Yeah," I said, "and it really sucks." I relayed bits and pieces of
last night's conversations, skipping over anything that had to do
with Daniel's arrest and upcoming trial.

"Sounds uncomfortable," he said when I finished.

"Yeah, that's a pretty good word for it." We were both quiet for
a minute. "So what's up with the speech club?"

"You mean our opportunity to join the NFL?"

"Huh?"

Vernon grinned and pushed his glasses up on his nose. "The
National Forensics League, of course. The NFL."

I laughed. "Right. Maybe that'll get my dad off my back about
sports. I can just tell him I'm in the NFL."

Chapter Five

"Well, you've got to start coming to practices first," Vernon said. "We have to earn points to become members, and we earn points at the meets. I have a booklet to give you. Yesterday the upperclassmen did demonstrations of the two types of debate and a couple of the interpretive readings."

"How was that?"

"Pretty cool. You can debate with a partner, or you can do it alone. I can't remember the names of them right now, though. They gave us this year's topics for the debates and guidelines for the interpretive stuff, and we're supposed to practice them. Next week they'll go over some of the other speeches, and we can start deciding which ones we'd like to prepare for."

I was having a hard time keeping my mind on debate.

"Hey, are you listening?" Vernon asked.

"Yeah, I'm sorry. Did you say how long we have to prepare?"

"Since the topics are assigned for the whole year, we've got plenty of time to polish our speeches and get as many sources as possible."

"We work on the same speech for a year before we give it?"

"No, no. Mr. Souza said we have several meets during the year. We're supposed to keep trying to perfect our speeches, so we'll kick ass at State. Our first meet is in three weeks," he said. "And it's on a Friday, which means we get out of school."

"I can handle that," I said, trying to be enthusiastic for Vernon. "So what are the topics for the year?"

"For the ones with partners, it's the minor's right to privacy. For the solo debates, it's the death penalty."

"Who all was there yesterday?"

"Let's see. Our sponsor, Mr. Souza, was there, obviously. But he said he leaves the sophomore training to our captains. Remember that guy from registration?"

"Arrogant wrestler dude?"

"Yeah. The guy named Pat. He's a captain. And remember that

cheerleader who was with him, Tess? She's the other one."

"What about the kids from the first meeting?"

Vernon wrinkled his forehead, trying to remember. "There were a lot more people at the practice yesterday, so I don't know."

"Really? How many?"

"I'm not sure. There were probably eight upperclassmen, but they don't have to come to the after-school practices, except for the captains. And I'd say there were about fifteen others."

"Wow. Sounds like a big group. Does everyone get to be in the meets?"

Vernon shrugged. "They didn't say. But they did say we have to be at the practice the week of a meet in order to be able to compete. And if we sign up to be in a meet and then don't show up, we have to pay the entrance fee. I've got this whole packet to give you," he repeated. "It's in my locker."

We were almost at school.

"So was that other girl there? You know, the one who sat way back in the corner?"

Vernon thought for a moment then shook his head. "I really can't remember. Tess asked about you, though."

"She what?"

"She asked me where you were."

"You're lying!"

"I'm serious," he insisted.

I cuffed him on the shoulder. "Why didn't you tell me that before?"

He grinned. "I wanted to see if you would ask about her."

The first bell rang as soon as we got to our lockers, so we split up to go to our classes.

At lunch, Vernon led me to a different table, where a few guys were already sitting. He introduced me to Ryan, Don, and Russ. I recognized Ryan from two of my classes. Vernon said that all three of them were joining the forensics team. Don tried to talk everyone into joining the chess club too.

At first I was a little uncomfortable, but the others talked so much, they didn't even notice I was being quiet. Don and Russ didn't stick around long. They wolfed down their food and then went off to use the computer lab.

"Hey," Ryan said. "A few of us are going to stay after school today and tomorrow to do some practice rounds. Want to come?"

Vernon bobbed his head enthusiastically.

"I can't today," I said. "I'll come tomorrow though. Where?"

"We'll meet in the same room we practice in, room 115. Mr. Souza doesn't care if we come practice in there as long as we leave when he does."

Just then, I happened to glance across the room. Without really thinking, I jumped up. "Be back in a minute," I said.

"Where's he going?" I heard Ryan ask.

I cut between the cafeteria tables. She was standing by the cash registers, holding her tray and looking around uncertainly.

"I didn't know you had lunch this hour," I said. Robin jumped a little, flinching away from me nervously. "Oh. It's you," she said. She continued to peer around the room. "I don't—I mean, I didn't. I had to get my schedule changed, and it took till today to get it all straightened out. Now I've got this lunch."

"Cool," I said.

"Not really. I don't know anybody who has this lunch."

"You know *me*," I began.

She rolled her eyes.

"No, really, I promise to be nice. You can come sit with us." She hesitated, and I added, "At least for today. Until you find someone else you want to sit with."

"Okay," she said finally. "Thanks."

She followed me across the cafeteria to where Vernon and Ryan were waiting. I pulled out a chair for her. She looked at me funny before she sat down, muttering something under her breath that I couldn't hear.

"In case you don't know them, these are other members of the forensics team," I said, introducing her.

She smiled and said hello, and then tried to turn her attention to her lunch. She barely got her fork to her mouth before Vernon and Ryan started firing questions at her.

"So what junior high did you go to?" Ryan asked.

"Who do you have for American lit?" Vernon wanted to know. "What hour? We must be in the same class."

"Do you have CP chemistry?"

"What are your electives?"

"What kind of books do you read?"

"Do you play any sports?"

Thank goodness for Vernon and Ryan. With their blunt questions, I learned more about Robin in five minutes than I knew about my own brother. I almost felt sorry for her, but she quickly turned the fire back on them and bombarded them with questions. And then she turned on me.

"So where were you yesterday?"

"Yesterday?"

"The forensics meeting? You said you were going to join, but you weren't there," she said to her apple before she took a bite.

"I couldn't make it," I said. "Family obligations." I smiled. "But I'll make sure I'm there next time."

"Some of us are going to practice today and tomorrow after school," Ryan cut in. "You can come if you like."

She thought about it for a minute. "I'll see what I can do."

The bell rang. Robin still hadn't finished her lunch. Ryan and Vernon got up, but I stayed where I was.

"Catch you later," I said to them.

Chapter Five

"See ya," they said as they joined the mass exodus out of the cafeteria.

"You don't have to wait."

"Sure I do. It's the polite thing to do."

"The polite thing? After your friends ask me so many questions I can't get three bites of food in, you're now going to sit there and stare at me while I try to eat? You consider that polite?"

I grinned and turned in my chair. "I won't stare," I said, looking in the other direction.

She shook her head and again muttered something that I couldn't catch. After a minute, she said, "So what was your family obligation?"

"Oh, nothing exciting," I said. Then, so I wouldn't sound like I was brushing her off, I asked, "What type of debate do you want to do? The one with a partner or the solo one?"

She sighed. "I'll do whatever they'll let me do in meets. I'd probably do better on my own, but I guess it'd be good for me to work with partners too. What about you?"

"I don't know. I haven't made up my mind."

"But you said you were coming next week."

"I'll probably give it a try," I said. "I'm not sure yet if this is for me."

"You don't want to compete?"

I shook my head. I wasn't sure I'd even be able to do a practice speech in front of my friends, but I didn't want to say that. Then she'd probably want to know why I was joining the team at all.

She pushed her chair back. "We better get going," she said, "or we'll be late."

I picked up her tray and emptied it into the trash can before stacking it. She was looking at me funny again. "What?" I asked.

"You pull out my chair, you clean up my tray... Are you a psycho, or are you the last gentleman left on the planet?"

I gave her a full smile. "I guess you'll have to get to know me better to find out."

"I was afraid you'd say that," she said as we got to the hall. "My locker's down this way, so I guess I'll see you later."

"How do you know my locker's not that way?"

She blushed as she said defiantly, "Well, is it?"

"No—but I think you already knew that." The hall suddenly seemed warmer.

Her blush deepened. "I've got to get going," she said quickly and turned to go.

"Yeah." My voice cracked, but I cleared my throat and kept talking. "Join us for lunch tomorrow if you want to."

She smiled and waved. I ran to my locker and then down the hall, slipping through the classroom door just as the late bell rang.

"Hello!" I called as I opened our front door. I didn't want a repeat of yesterday. "Hello?" I yelled again when there was no answer.

I dropped my backpack on the floor and went out to check the garage. It was empty.

"Terrific. I come straight home to be here for Daniel, and he's not even here," I muttered to myself, grabbing a Coke and a bag of chips from the kitchen.

It took me less than an hour to finish my homework, and since I had finished my library book the night before, I had nothing else to do. I was watching TV when Dad got home a little after five. "How was your day?" he asked on his way from the garage to his room.

I waited the five minutes it took for him to change into jeans and a T-shirt and come back to the living room. "It was fine. How was yours?"

"It was all right. You get all caught up from yesterday?"

"Yeah."

"Was your friend able to fill you in on that speech stuff?"

"Yeah. A few of us are going to practice after school tomorrow."

"Good," he mumbled absently as he flipped through the mail.

"I thought you might come home early today."

"Oh? Why's that?"

"Since you left so early this morning," I said.

"Nope," he said, taking the bills to the office. "Just had a lot to do today." He came back and glanced at the clock. "Dan's not back yet?"

I shook my head. "I'm the only one here."

Dad frowned. "I didn't think his appointment with the lawyer would take so long. I wish he had let one of us go with him."

He got a Coke from the kitchen and joined me on the couch, watching the news. Mom got home fifteen minutes later.

"Hello!" she called from the front door. "Sorry I'm late!" She came into the living room with a puzzled look on her face. "Where's Daniel?"

"Maclean's secretary said he could work him in around three," Dad said.

"The appointment wouldn't take this long, would it?" She didn't give him a chance to answer before she turned to me. "Has he called?"

"No," I said.

"That's strange. Well," she said, "I'm sure he'll be home in time for dinner. I told him six-thirty. Shadow, will you get out the chicken and some frozen vegetables while I change?" She started down the hall without stopping to kiss Dad hello the way she usually did.

"Sure." I got up and went to the kitchen.

Mom joined me a few minutes later. She had me set the table and then shooed me out, claiming I was in her way.

The six o'clock news ended. Dad and I stayed in the living room, watching a game show. The smells coming from the kitchen made my stomach rumble loudly.

At quarter till seven, Mom came in and sat down. No one said anything. She and Dad didn't even look at each other. They just stared fixedly at the TV. The tension in the house seemed to increase every minute.

Half an hour later, my stomach growled again, even louder this time.

"Is dinner ready?" Dad asked.

Mom gave a quick nod.

"Maybe we should go ahead and eat."

"He'll be here. We can wait."

"How long do you plan on waiting, Caroline?"

"He'll be here!" she snapped.

During the next commercial I hesitantly asked, "What happens if he doesn't come back?"

Mom made a small noise in the back of her throat. She stood up quickly. "I can't believe…you don't…" Finally she blurted out, "Fine, go ahead and eat!"

She started out of the living room. Dad stood up and tried to stop her, but she pushed him away and ran down the hall.

He bowed his head down for a moment and then turned to me. "I guess it's just the two of us for dinner."

We fixed our plates in silence. Dad started toward the table, then stopped, looking at the four empty chairs surrounding the table. "What do you say we just eat on the couch tonight?"

"Sounds good."

While we ate, a reality show rerun came on; neither of us bothered to change the channel.

"I didn't mean to upset Mom," I said.

Dad sighed. "It's okay, Shadow. It's like I told you, this isn't easy for any of us." He was quiet for a few minutes. "The night Daniel left, it was my decision to come down hard on him. Your mother thought I was being too strict. We had discussed punishment several times before, but she was always against it. She thought that he was just going through a phase, that he'd snap out of it. I went along with her decision, until that night, when I had had enough." Staring at his empty plate, he shook his head. "For a long time, I blamed myself for Daniel leaving. It was easy to feel guilty, because every time I looked at your mother, I knew she was blaming me too."

"Dad..." I began, but I had no idea what to say. He had never talked to me about that night.

"So now," he continued, "Daniel's come home. And your mother doesn't want anyone to refuse him anything, because she doesn't want to lose him again."

"But we have to have him back before we can lose him," I muttered.

Dad flashed me a sad grin. "You've always been an insightful kid." He paused, then quietly added, "Your mother thinks he's back."

"He's here, but he doesn't act like he plans to stay."

"I'm afraid he doesn't. When he called, he said he just wanted to let us know he was alive and okay. He didn't ask us to bail him out, and he didn't ask if he could come home. Your mother just took over."

"How much was the bail?" I had been curious, but there hadn't been a good time to ask until now.

"More than we can afford to lose."

"We might lose it?"

"If Daniel skips town."

"Do you think he will?"

Dad shrugged. "As you pointed out the night he called, we don't really know him anymore. But the judge was willing to set bail for two reasons. One, he's never been arrested before. And two, we agreed to be responsible for him."

"Is that why you didn't want him to use a car?"

"That's part of it. The other part is that I don't know how well he drives. I don't even know if he has a license."

"So why did Mom give him her car?"

"He's her baby, Shadow, the same way you are. And she doesn't want anything to hurt either of you. For the last seven years, she hasn't been able to do anything for Daniel, so she wants to make up for it now. She wants to give him everything. I'm already looking like the bad guy, already saying no to him." Dad sighed and ran his hand through his hair. "I'd like to know what he's been doing these last years, because that might explain a lot, but he won't talk about it and your mother won't press the issue. She doesn't want to upset him."

"She doesn't want to upset him?" I asked. "Or she doesn't want to be upset by what she hears?"

Dad looked at me but didn't say anything.

I started gathering the dishes. As I headed to the kitchen, Dad stood up. "I'll go check on your mother. These next few weeks are going to be hard, Shadow, for everyone."

I had never seen my father look so old, so tired.

It took Dad a while, but he finally talked Mom into coming back into the living room. She jumped every time the clock chimed, and when the phone rang a little before nine, she raced for it. It was a wrong number. A few minutes later, it was Vernon.

As she handed me the phone, she covered the mouthpiece and said, "No more than five minutes. We have to keep the line clear."

Vernon wanted to know if I had written down the page numbers for our chemistry assignment. It took me a few seconds to find the right page in my notebook. After I read the numbers out to him, I lowered my voice a little. "So Robin's in your American lit class, huh?"

"Yeah. I didn't realize it before, because she sits a few rows over and behind me. Besides, she's good at making herself invisible."

"You mean she's quiet in class?"

"Well, yeah. Seems to me she's pretty quiet everywhere. She hardly talked at all during lunch."

Mom cleared her throat loudly. I glanced at her and she gave me an impatient look.

I turned around and walked a couple of feet down the hall. "What do you mean? Robin talked a lot today. You guys didn't give her a chance to be quiet. You asked her so many questions she couldn't even eat her lunch!"

Vernon laughed. "I guess that's true. Is she in any of your classes?"

Before I could respond, Mom snapped, "Shadow, your five minutes are up!"

I went back to the living room and sat down, phone to my ear. She stood up, hands on her hips, glaring at me. I glared right back.

"Just a second!" I said.

"You've had your second! Hang up the phone!"

"Hey, man, I've got to get going anyway," Vernon said.

"You sure?"

"Yeah. See you tomorrow morning."

"See ya."

I hung up.

"Thank you!" Mom said. I handed her the phone and sank further into my chair. She returned to the sofa, clutching the phone.

The garage door finally opened a little after nine. Mom ran out to meet Daniel. Dad and I exchanged glances, but neither of us moved.

A few minutes later, the two of them came in together. Daniel carried in two six-packs of beer and put them in the fridge on his way to the living room. Mom was hovering behind him.

"Hey," Daniel said easily. "Sorry I'm late. Lost track of time."

Even from across the room, I could smell the cigarette smoke.

"Where were you?" Dad asked. His face was blank, his tone bland.

"I stopped at JR Rocker's on the way back from the lawyer."

Mom jumped in eagerly. "How did the meeting go?"

Daniel shrugged. "Fine. I still don't think we need this guy, though. The case is going to be the same if you pay for a fancy lawyer or if the state just pays for a public defender."

"Oh, no," Mom said. "Mr. Maclean is the best lawyer in town. I'm sure—"

"Something smells good," Daniel cut in. "Is there any left?"

"Of course," Mom said, bustling off to the kitchen. "Sit down and I'll get you a plate."

"Anything good on the tube?" Daniel asked, flopping down in a chair.

I picked up the remote. "We're watching a movie," I said, turning the volume up a notch. I kept the remote in my hand.

"So, what else did you do today?" Dad asked.

"Nothing, really. Just went to that meeting and then to the bar."

"How long did the meeting take?"

"About forty-five minutes."

That meant he had been at Rocker's from around four o'clock till almost nine. I could tell Dad was thinking the same thing I was.

Mom brought the plate of food out for him, along with one of the beers. "Here you go, honey."

"Thanks." He smiled up at her. "Looks great."

"Aren't you going to eat, Mom?" I asked.

She shook her head, smiling, without taking her eyes off Daniel. "I'm not hungry."

"Hey," Daniel stopped shoveling food in his mouth and swallowed. "Can I use your car again tomorrow?"

"No!" Dad said immediately.

"Mark—"

"Caroline, he's just driven himself home in our car after spending nearly five hours in a bar! He could've ki— " Dad broke off, but we all knew what he had been about to say. His face turned so red it was almost purple.

"Hey, Dad, I'm not entirely stupid," Daniel said with a weak grin. "I wasn't drinking."

Dad raised an eyebrow.

"I wasn't drinking before I drove," Daniel amended. "I had two beers the whole time I was there. Swear to God."

Dad was watching Mom. She glanced at him and he shook his head. She looked back at Daniel and sighed. "Yes, you can use the car tomorrow, but that will be the last time for a while. I've got a busy schedule coming up at work."

Dad closed his eyes.

"Thanks, Mom."

"You've got to be home by five though. And no drinking!"

I excused myself and went to hide in my room. I thought about calling Vernon back, but I was afraid it might be too late. I dug through my old books and found a favorite I hadn't read in a while and climbed into bed with it.

A few minutes later, there was a knock at my door. "Yeah," I said, thinking it would be Dad. It was Daniel.

"Hey, man. What's up?"

"What do you want?" I asked suspiciously.

"Just want to talk," he said, wandering over to the shelves by the window. He picked up an old model Mustang, turned it over in his hands, and put it back.

"I never got another piggy bank," I said, "if that's what you're looking for."

"Is that why you've been so pissy to me? Just 'cause I took some of your change seven years ago?"

I thought he wouldn't remember what I was talking about. For him to admit to the theft so callously only made me mad all over again. "No, Daniel, you didn't just take some of my change. You took all the money I had saved. So why don't you just leave?"

He sighed. "I came in here to make up, Shadow." He reached in his back pocket and pulled out a wad of bills. "Here. This should take care of my debt."

My anger shifted to fear. "How'd you get that? Dad said you didn't have any money."

He shrugged easily. "I know how to make money. It's one of the things you have to learn when you're living on the street." He paused. "I'll tell you where I got it if you really want to know."

I did. I really did want to know all about him, but a cowardly part of me was afraid to find out. I guess Mom wasn't the only one who was afraid of being upset by hearing what he had to say.

"Look," I said uncomfortably, "it's late. I've got to get up early tomorrow."

"Sure," Daniel said. "Where do you want this?" He waved the bills around.

"Keep it," I said. "You didn't take that much."

"Oh, consider this interest," he said, flashing a big grin. I had forgotten that he had two dimples.

"I don't want it," I said. And it was true. I had never really cared that he had taken the money from me. I would have given it to him if he had asked. It was that he had taken himself and my trust away too.

He walked over to my desk, picked up my backpack, and slipped the folded bills inside a side pocket. "In case of an emergency," he told me, winking. He walked out of my room and shut the door behind him.

As tired as I was, I lay awake for a long time.

Chapter Six

The next afternoon, I went to the voluntary forensics practice. Of the eight people there, Vernon, Ryan, and Russ were the only ones I knew. Vernon introduced me to two girls, Erica and Lia. I was disappointed that Robin didn't show up. A couple of guys came in late to work on their own interpretive speeches and didn't talk to us much.

The rest of us practiced debates. We decided to do a Cross-Examination debate first, and then try Lincoln-Douglas debates if we had time. The CX debates involve partners, and the L-D debates are done solo. Since Erica and I had missed the official practice on Wednesday, we were the judges. Mr. Souza gave us a box of debate topics and a CX debate ballot so we could mark the scores. Vernon paired up with Lia for the affirmative side, and that left Russ and Ryan on the negative team.

I drew a debate topic from the box and Erica read it to the team. "Resolved: The U.S. needs to change its foreign policy with China."

"How much time do we get to prepare?" Russ asked.

I looked at the guidelines. "It says here you get ten minutes to prepare opening speeches, and then five minutes per team before your speeches during the debate."

The two teams went to the file cabinets, looking for articles relating to the debate topic. Apparently the forensics team kept files on everything from toxic waste to cloning to affirmative action laws. Vernon said we were all expected to help keep the files current by bringing in new articles on different issues. They also maintained a list of active websites and message boards.

The CX ballot broke down pretty clearly what was expected from the debaters and gave us the scale for judging them. I had read the information Vernon had given me, but Erica said she hadn't looked at her stuff yet. We went through the ballot together, and I explained what I could to her.

"Wow," she said, looking at the times.

"What?"

"They get an hour for speaking," she said, pointing to the alternating speaking schedule. "And that doesn't include the time they can stop to prepare. I don't think we're going to have time to practice much else today."

We settled in for the debate. It was hard work for all of us. Vernon seemed nervous, even though he knew everyone in the room. Russ spoke too fast, and Ryan wouldn't look up from his notes at all. Lia really seemed to enjoy being the center of attention, but she went over her allotted time each time she spoke. Erica and I had a hard time keeping track of the time, and we messed up twice. The whole debate took us an hour and twenty minutes. Through it all, Mr. Souza sat at his desk, grading papers. At least, that's what I thought he was doing.

"That was impressive," he said as we began gathering our things, "but next time you might want to do just the first half of the debate and really tighten up your speeches. At practice, it's okay to stop speakers, give them some pointers, and then have them start over. It's a lot easier than trying to remember everything that's been said in the last hour." He smiled at Erica and me.

Chapter Six

"I usually don't stay more than an hour after school, but it was worth it to stay a little later today. I don't often have a group of sophomores come in on their own to practice a CX debate the first week of school. It can be a little overwhelming for beginners unless there's an upperclassman involved. I hope you all can maintain this level of energy and dedication for the year." He flipped through the stack of papers. "Let's see. Vernon. Lia. Ryan. Russ." He handed each one of them a sheet. "These are just some of my notes and observations. I thought they might help."

They looked at each other in surprise and murmured their thanks.

"Will you help us with the Lincoln-Douglas debate on Monday?" Vernon asked.

Mr. Souza grinned. "Why don't you all take Monday off? I'll make sure at least one of the upperclassmen comes in to help on Tuesday."

We nodded in agreement and began filing out the door.

"Have a good weekend, Mr. Souza," Russ said.

"You too."

The girls stayed behind so Lia could talk with Mr. Souza about her evaluation sheet. Vernon, Ryan, Russ, and I headed down the deserted halls.

Russ was pumped up about the comments Mr. Souza had given him. Ryan was a little bummed about his. After they had finished comparing notes, Vernon suggested we all go out and do something over the weekend.

"Yeah!" Russ bobbed his head. "Let me get your number." He pulled a scrap of paper out of his pocket. "Anyone have a pen?"

"I do," I said, swinging my backpack around and fumbling with the front pocket. Out of the corner of my eye, I sensed movement, and glanced up to see Mr. Barnett stepping out of his office. My hand found a pen, and as I pulled it out, the wad of bills fell to the ground. Right at Mr. Barnett's feet.

He bent down, scooped up the money, and looked at us in surprise. "Mr. Shadow. Gentlemen. You're here late today."

"Forensics practice," Ryan said.

"I thought that was on Wednesdays."

"It is," Russ said, "but those of us just starting need some extra help."

"I see. And how are things going for you, Mr. Shadow?" He turned his sharp eyes to me. "Any more problems with the alarm clock?"

"Nope," I said, shaking my head.

"And this is yours?" he asked, waving the roll of money as he pulled his walkie-talkie off his belt with his other hand. "Mr. Morse," he said into it, "could you please meet me at the office?"

"Right there," the radio crackled back.

Vernon and I exchanged glances.

"Shadow?" Vernon whispered. "Is that yours?"

I nodded.

We all just stood there silently in a loose circle for almost a minute before Mr. Morse, one of the campus security guards, came around the corner.

"What's going on?" he said, smiling but obviously sizing us all up.

Wordlessly, Mr. Barnett handed him the money.

Mr. Morse flipped the folded bills open and sniffed them. He looked at Mr. Barnett, then turned to us. "Whose is this?" he asked.

"Mine," I said.

"Do you mind if I take a look at your backpack?" Mr. Morse said easily.

"Why?"

"Just want to make sure you're not carrying anything on school grounds that you shouldn't be."

I just stood there.

"You don't have to give it to me," Mr. Morse said. "We could step in the office and wait until your parents and the sheriff show up instead."

"For what?" Russ said indignantly. "We're just going home."

"Late, very late. And with a large amount of money. This is probable cause in the world of narcotics."

I handed my backpack over to him, and he rummaged through it. "Got anything in your pockets, big guy?"

Instead of answering, I pulled my pockets inside out. He finished inspecting the bag and then handed it back to me.

"You sell very often?"

"Sell what?" I asked, confused.

Mr. Morse looked at me for a long second, and I could feel him weighing my answer in his mind. He smelled the bills one more time, and then shook his head at Mr. Barnett.

"Can he have his money now?" Russ demanded.

"Sure," Mr. Morse said, refolding the bills. As he held them out, he said, "You probably shouldn't bring that much to school. You know we're not responsible for anything that's stolen from lockers or backpacks."

"I'll be sure to remember that," I said, relieved that my hand didn't shake as I took the money.

"What are you doing carrying so much cash at school?"

I shrugged. "It's not that much," I said, although I had no idea how much was really there.

Mr. Morse raised his eyebrows. "Not that much? Maybe you could just give it to me, then."

Russ and Vernon chuckled nervously.

He studied my face for a moment. "Are you related to Daniel Thompson?" he asked.

Through stiff lips, I managed to say, "He's my brother."

"Has your family heard from him?" Mr. Barnett put a caring and concerned expression on his face.

"Yeah." That was all I said. I wasn't going to let him rattle me anymore.

"I saw a Daniel Thompson mentioned in the Denver paper, about a month ago, wasn't it?" Mr. Barnett glanced at Mr. Morse, then back at me. "Was that him?"

So much for not letting him rattle me. My stomach seemed to have frozen inside me. I couldn't think of a thing to say.

"Nah," Vernon said after a few seconds of my silence. "If Shadow had a famous brother, he would have told everyone."

"Good," he said, turning to Vernon. "And you're Glenn Thomas's brother, aren't you?"

"Yeah," Vernon mumbled, not looking at Mr. Barnett.

"How's he doing? What's he up to?"

"He's taking some courses at the community college," Vernon said, "and working a part-time job."

Mr. Barnett nodded as if that's what he expected to hear. "Tell him I said hello."

"Uh-huh," Vernon said.

"Okay, gentlemen. Enjoy your weekend. And stay out of trouble." He and Mr. Morse turned and headed down the hallway, talking quietly.

None of us said anything until we were outside.

"'Tell him I said hello,'" Vernon mimicked. "Yeah, I will, when I want to wreck his day! My brother hated Mr. Barnett!"

"Watch yourself now," Russ warned. "If he didn't get along with your brother, he might take it out on you."

"I'll just stay out of his way."

I pulled the bills out of my back pocket and sniffed them. Ryan watched with interest.

"What's it smell like?" he asked.

"Nothing." I smelled again. "Cigarettes, maybe…" I sniffed one more time. "No. Never mind. Just nothing."

"Why'd he smell it?" Ryan wondered out loud.

Russ laughed and shook his head at him. "To see if it smelled like dope, you dope!"

Vernon was laughing too, but he stopped suddenly. "Really?" he asked.

I was quiet. Daniel had only gone to school here for a year, but Mr. Morse had remembered him—remembered him enough to put us together.

"From what I hear, everyone hates Mr. Barnett," Ryan said. Then he turned to me. "What did he mean about your brother?"

"My brother ran away from home a week before his junior year began," I said simply.

"How long was he gone?" Russ asked.

I hesitated.

"He was gone for a while, but then he came back," Vernon said, saving me once again. "It's no big deal."

When we came to the corner, we split up, because Ryan and Russ lived in a different neighborhood.

"See ya Monday," Russ said.

"See ya," Ryan echoed.

"Later." Vernon waved at them. I stayed quiet.

After a few minutes, I cleared my throat. "Thanks, man."

He waved it off. "Like I said, it's no big deal."

"Actually, it kind of is. You may have just lied to Barnett for me."

"What do you mean?"

I took a deep breath. "My brother has to go to court in a few weeks."

"What for?"

"He's been charged with homicide."

Vernon stopped short. "I'm sorry...did you just say—"

"Yep." I kept walking.

Vernon trotted to catch up with me. "Homicide? As in a dead body?"

"Yep."

After a moment, Vernon whistled low. "Wow. I guess that's why you weren't too crazy to see him when he got back, huh?"

"Pretty much."

Vernon hesitated. "Did he do it?" he asked.

"I don't know."

A few more minutes of silence, and then Vernon asked, "Do you think he did?"

"I don't know."

Daniel wasn't home when I got there. I headed straight down the hall toward the bedrooms. I knew I only had a few minutes before Dad would be coming in from work.

The door to Daniel's room was shut. It had been left open for so long, reminding us all of its emptiness, that I was almost afraid to turn the knob. As it swung open, it revealed a room different from the one I remembered. All the posters were off the walls. There were several paper bags stacked by the wall, and I saw the rolled posters sticking out of one of them.

Walking over, I discovered that the other bags were full of his CDs and neatly folded old clothing. He was cleaning everything out. Now it didn't look like Daniel had ever lived there. It looked like a guestroom.

I scanned the room again. There had to be a place where I could leave the money, a place where he would find it.

Then, sticking out of a pocket of the khaki pants he had worn the night before, something green caught my eye. It was another wad of bills. Most of them were ones and fives, but there were at least a couple of twenties too. Quickly I shoved the money he had given me in the other pants pocket. He would find it there, but hopefully he wouldn't realize I had returned his payment, including the interest.

Chapter Six

I left the room as fast as I could. I was afraid of what else I might find in there.

Mom and Dad came home from work together. Apparently he had picked her up, instead of having her wait for her friend. She also had a bouquet of flowers in her hand, but they were arguing.

"Caroline, we have to present him with a united front. We can't let him play us off each other."

"We tried the united front before, and it drove him away."

"So you're willing to let him destroy our family?"

"Mark!" Mom exclaimed, looking pointedly at me. "We'll talk about this later."

"It's okay," I said, even though it really wasn't. "I know you guys fight."

"We don't fight, Shadow," Mom said soothingly. "We just disagree sometimes."

"Mom, I'm not a baby. It's fighting."

"No, it's not. It's—"

"This one is going to be a fight if we don't get some things settled," Dad muttered.

Mom glared at him and headed for their bedroom. Dad sighed and shook his head as he flipped through the mail.

"Dad, how much money did you say Daniel had?"

He glanced up at me. "He didn't have any, but I think your mother gave him money for some new clothes before she left for work yesterday."

"Oh," I said. I looked in the fridge for something to munch on. "Why?"

For a moment I thought about telling him. I knew he already felt left out of what was going on in the house. But at the same time, I didn't want to cause more tension by putting him in another awkward position. "Just wondering."

"Is he home yet?"

"Nope."

Dad sighed again and then headed to their bedroom.

I took my soda to the living room, and Mom joined me. She must have passed Dad in the hall.

"How was your day?" I asked her.

"Fine," she replied absently. "Where's Daniel?"

I shrugged.

Dad came back, in jeans and a T-shirt. Mom *tsk*ed and shook her head. "What?" Dad asked.

"I told you I thought we should go out to dinner tonight." She was still wearing her skirt and blouse.

"I didn't realize you meant someplace dressy," Dad said. He sat down on the couch.

"You'll have to change."

Dad picked up the remote. "When Daniel gets home for dinner, I'll change. We have no idea when that will be."

He clicked the TV on, which was good, because he had just clicked the conversation off.

Daniel wasn't exactly on time for dinner, but he wasn't three and a half hours late, either. He came strolling in at seven-fifteen, carrying a bag of groceries.

"Hello!" he called cheerfully as he came in the door. "Is anybody hungry?"

"Yeah, but that's because we usually eat at six-thirty," I said.

"Shadow!" Mom hissed at me. Dad hid a grin.

"I've got dinner, but I'm going to need a little help cooking it," my brother said, coming out of the kitchen.

"Well, actually, we were going to…" Mom began, but then she just smiled. "I'd love to help you cook. What did you get?"

"Potatoes, salad, and lobster tails!"

For a second, Mom and Dad just looked at him. They both spoke at the same time. "That sounds wonderful," Mom said,

Chapter Six

while Dad was demanding, "Where did you get the money for all that?"

Daniel looked hurt. "Mom slipped me a little just-in-case cash yesterday. I didn't use any of it, so I thought I'd get us dinner."

Dad clearly didn't believe him. He opened his mouth, but Mom shot him a look and he closed it again. I chewed on my lip. My brother certainly had plenty of cash lying around in his room, and I was pretty sure he had more in his pockets right now. But I didn't say anything.

"Just give me a minute to get changed, and I'll start dinner," Mom said, kissing Daniel on the cheek as she left the room.

Dad cleared his throat. "You did hear your mom ask you to be home at five, didn't you?"

"Sorry," Daniel said. "I'll try not to be late again."

I returned to the couch, and Daniel took what had already become his chair.

"Man, who died?" he asked me.

"What?"

"Who died?" he repeated. "What's with all the black? It's all you've been wearing this week."

Mom came back through the living room just in time to hear. "That's been his thing for the last couple of years," she said, shaking her head. "I've tried talking him out of it, but he insists. Maybe you'll have better luck."

Daniel raised his eyebrows at me. "It makes you look sick."

"Thanks, Daniel," I said dryly.

"It's Dan."

"Well, Dan, thanks for sharing your opinion. I'm overcome with the need to go put on a bright blue shirt and green pants right now."

"No, seriously, it makes you look sick and pale."

I shook my head and kept my eyes on the TV.

"You could use a haircut too."

I stared at him in disbelief. "What?"

"You look like some kind of troublemaker, with your hair all long and wearing all black like that. You should clean yourself up, try to look good."

I was pissed. "Why do I need to look good?" I demanded. "I'm the one who stayed in school. I'm the one on the honor roll. You might look all 'clean' and 'good,' but you're the criminal! Why would I want to look like you?"

Dad put a hand on my arm. I jerked away from him. "Come on, Shadow," he said, gentle and firm at the same time. "Take it easy."

"I don't want to take it easy," I said. "What right does this convict have to—"

Mom came out of the kitchen. "Shadow!" she yelled, hands on her hips.

"What?" I asked her. "What right does he have to come in here and judge me when he doesn't even know who I am? What right does he have to criticize anyone when he's been arrested for murder?"

"Shadow!" Mom said sharply. "I think you've said enough."

"Just not saying something doesn't make it go away, Mom." I plowed on. "He left this family a long time ago and now he's been arrested. Those are the facts. He's got no right to blow back in here and start criticizing when we eat, what I wear, or anything else!"

"I think you should go to your room to cool off," she said.

"Fine," I said, standing up. "I'd rather be there anyway!"

"You can come back when you're ready to apologize."

"Caroline," Dad began.

"Then I won't be coming back," I told her flatly. "He owes me an apology, and he owes you and Dad an apology. But you're so concerned with keeping him happy that you don't care about anyone else's feelings now. Not even the people who have actually been here to care about you!"

Chapter Six

When I got to my room, it was all I could do to keep from slamming the door shut. I could hear their voices through the wall. I turned my stereo up so I wouldn't have to listen to them.

I flopped down on my bed. A few minutes later, I heard a knock on my door. "Go away," I said. Someone knocked again. "What?" Another knock. "Okay, okay, come in already!"

Daniel stuck his head in. "Come on back, Shadow," he said.

"No thanks. I'm fine here."

"Look, I'm sorry about what I said. You were right. I shouldn't have dissed you."

I didn't say anything, just scowled at the ceiling.

"I'm sorry things are so weird. I just…I just don't know how to act around you guys. I don't know what to say and when I try to talk it all comes out wrong. That's why I got the lobster. I wanted to apologize."

"Oh, what a nice apology. Come home late, and 'Oh, by the way, Mom, I brought stuff for you to cook for me.'"

"Shadow, I'm sorry! I'm just not used to how things work around here."

"And whose fault it that?"

"Mine," he said simply. "And if you don't think I've been paying for it for a long time, you're a fool…even if you are on the honor roll." He sighed. "Look, I'm trying, okay? Could you at least try too?"

That was almost exactly what Mom had said. Why didn't anyone think I was trying?

"Come back out to the living room, Shadow. I promise to lay off."

I still didn't say anything. He backed out and shut the door. I waited a few minutes, trying to gauge how long I could stay in my room before one of my parents came to chase me out.

Finally, I got up. I met Dad in the hall as I stepped out of my room.

"Coming to join us?" he asked.

"Coming to get me?"

"No," he said. "Just going to the bathroom."

I didn't believe him, but how do you accuse someone of lying about that? "See you in a few minutes then."

Daniel didn't look over when I came in and sat down on the couch. A few minutes later, Mom stuck her head in to tell us to move to the dining room for dinner. I knew she was disappointed and frustrated with me, but at least she didn't say anything.

After dinner, while Dad and I did dishes, Mom and Daniel ran out to rent a movie. The movie was Daniel's suggestion. It irked me that even though this extravagant dinner had supposedly been his way to say thank you, he hadn't done any of the work. He was still acting like a guest.

"Shadow, for what it's worth, I agreed with you earlier," Dad said. "I don't think Daniel's in a position to criticize much of anything right now."

I glanced at him out of the corner of my eye. "Even though you agreed with what he was saying?"

Dad grimaced. "You know your mother and I aren't crazy about the way you dress, and I've never approved of your long hair. However, that's not the point. I didn't agree with the way he was saying it, or the reasons."

"Mom didn't seem to think it made a difference."

He sighed. "I tried to explain to you the other night, Shadow, how hard this is on all of us. But it's even more difficult for your mother. She's terrified of losing him again."

"Are you?"

"Yeah."

"But you're not all wigged out about it."

He smiled. "I guess I hide it well. But believe me, inside, I'm very wigged out."

"I just don't get it. He screwed up big time, and he keeps screwing up while he's here, but she yells at me instead."

"There are times when she'd like to yell at him, but she doesn't want to drive him away. So she's yelling at you—and at me too. It's not very fair, but there it is."

"Yeah, well maybe I should run away too."

"Shadow, don't even joke about that! Your mother still loves you very much, and if she ever thought she might lose you... I don't even want to think about what would happen."

We finished the dishes in silence, and then waited for Mom and Daniel in the living room.

"Hey, Dad. Did Daniel get in a lot of trouble with Mr. Morse at school?"

Dad blinked. "Daniel got in quite a bit of trouble with just about everyone at the end of his sophomore year. Why?"

I shrugged. "Mr. Morse asked me about him today."

"That last semester, Daniel skipped a lot of classes. One of the administrators gave him detention for it several times, and finally in-school suspension, but it didn't stop Daniel. A couple of times they asked us to come in for a conference, but..."

"But what?"

"Your mother—she and I—we didn't realize how bad it was. We thought we could handle the problems with Daniel at home."

"Was he in the paper?"

"What?

"Was there an article about Daniel and the murder in the paper?"

"I haven't seen one. Why?"

"Just wondering if his case was getting much media attention."

"Not that I know of. Not here. Not yet."

I didn't get to ask him anything else, because right then Mom and Daniel came in together, laughing. On the way home from the movie rental store, they had stopped and picked up ice cream sundaes for all of us.

We ate our ice cream in the living room, sampling from each other's flavors, and started the movie. Although we didn't talk much while we watched the video, it was the most comfortable evening we had spent since that phone call.

We were almost like a normal family.

Chapter Seven

On Saturday, I slept in until almost ten. Usually my parents wake me up by nine, because they don't like to see me waste the whole morning in bed.

After I showered, I went out to the kitchen. Mom was sitting at the dining room table, going through some papers.

"Morning," I said.

She looked up. "Good morning, honey."

I started to get some cereal.

"I'll be making pancakes, if you want to wait until your brother gets up."

I hesitated. She hadn't made pancakes for breakfast in months. "No, thanks. I'm really hungry right now."

I poured the milk over my cereal, got a spoon, and started to head to the living room.

"Why don't you eat in here?" Mom suggested.

I couldn't think of a reasonable objection. "Okay."

I sat down at the table across from her and began to eat. "What are you doing?" I asked, glancing at the various bank statements she had in front of her.

"Just catching up on bills and finances," she said distractedly.

I stirred my cereal. I wasn't really hungry anymore, but if I didn't eat it, Mom would think something was wrong.

"How did the meeting with the lawyer go?"

"I don't know," she said. "Dan didn't want to talk about it."

"Couldn't you call the lawyer?"

"I can't do that. Lawyer-client confidentiality."

"Even though you're paying for it?"

"Um-hmm." She was still flipping through papers, looking for something.

"But you and Dad got this expensive lawyer for him. He could at least tell you what's going on."

"He's an adult, Shadow." She sighed. "But he's our son—your brother. We have to help him however we can."

She's still afraid to know what happened, I thought. "Where's Dad?" I asked.

"He went in to the office for a little bit."

"He what?" I stared at her. I couldn't remember Dad ever going in to work on a Saturday.

"He's got a lot of work this week."

"I guess," I said, not making any effort to keep the sarcasm out of my voice. "He went in early twice this week and now today. He *must* be busy. It's not like we've got any problems at home that he'd be avoiding."

She slammed her hand down on the table, and it was so unexpected that I probably jumped a good six inches into the air. "I don't know what you're trying to imply, but I do not like the tone of your voice, young man!"

I thought about asking if she wanted me to draw her a picture, but then I took another look at her anger-flushed cheeks and decided against it. Instead, I pushed back from the table and picked up the bowl.

"Where are you going?" she asked as she picked up the phone.

"To my room to finish my homework."

"Keep your stereo down, please. Dan's still sleeping."

I clenched my teeth and put my dishes in the dishwasher.

Chapter Seven

As I walked down the hall, I heard Mom saying, "Yes, I was calling to find out the penalty for early withdrawal on a CD, and what your interest rates on loans are right now."

I turned on my stereo as soon as I was in my room, controlling the urge to turn the volume way up. It only took me twenty minutes to finish my homework, but I didn't feel like going back out to the kitchen or living room. I decided to clean my room. I tore it apart first, digging through drawers and shelves, pulling everything out and checking each item. I made one stack of things to keep and another one of things to throw out. Before I knew it, almost three hours had passed. I was starving.

Stepping out in the hall, I glanced down to Daniel's room. The door was still shut.

Mom was sitting on the couch, reading. She looked up as I came in, and gave me a weak smile. "You must have had a lot of homework."

"Actually, I barely had any."

"So what have you been doing in there?"

"Cleaning out my desk and book shelves."

"That's a big job. How far did you get?"

"I'm finished."

She raised her eyebrows. "You cleaned everything out?"

"Uh-huh."

In the kitchen, I began pulling out stuff to make sandwiches.

Mom called in, "We'll be going out to lunch in a little bit, if you can wait. Otherwise, just have a snack."

I stuck my head back in the living room. "How soon is a little bit?"

"As soon as Daniel gets up."

"He's still asleep?"

She nodded.

"Good thing I didn't wait for pancakes," I muttered, going back into the kitchen.

I made myself two sandwiches and grabbed an apple. When I turned to go into the dining room, there was Mom in the doorway, watching me with a frown.

"That looks like more than a snack," she said.

"I'm hungry," I said. "And who knows how long Daniel will sleep."

"I'm sure he'll be up soon."

"You said that a few hours ago," I pointed out as I set my lunch on the table.

She gave me one of those looks that let me know she was upset with me, but she didn't say anything.

I went back to the fridge to get a soda, and she was still staring at me. "What?"

"We'll be going out soon," she repeated.

"Where are you going?"

"We're going shopping. And I want you to come with us."

"Why?"

"So we can all be together."

"I don't need anything."

"I'd like you to come with us," she repeated, raising her voice just a little.

"Mom, I hate the mall, I don't need anything, and I've got other things to do. I'm not going."

"Don't use that tone of voice with me! I'm not asking if you want to come, I'm telling you that you're coming with us."

"Why?"

"Because it will be good for you to spend time with Daniel."

"I spent enough time with him for the last two nights. I need to go to the library today."

"You can go to the library later this week."

"No!" I suddenly shouted. "You keep pushing back everything that I want to do!"

"Shadow, you said you would try—" she began.

"And I have tried. But I'm not going to spend every minute with him!"

"He's only been here a few days—"

"I know. And I've rearranged my entire life for him because you asked me to, but today I've got stuff I need to do. Maybe if he decides to stick around, I'll spend more time with him."

"I know you've been an only child for a while, Shadow, but there's no reason to be this selfish. You're acting like a spoiled brat."

I wanted to scream. She really just didn't see what she was doing. Shaking my head, I grabbed my two sandwiches and my soda and headed out the back door.

"Where do you think you're going?"

"I'm going to the library. I'll be back later."

"Young man, you get back here!"

I stepped off the back porch and went to the gate. I looked up at the gray sky, and hoped it wouldn't decide to rain on me. I had left my jacket in my room, but I wasn't about to go back and get it. The way she had shouted at me, I half expected her to come chasing after me. She didn't.

The library was calm and quiet, which was exactly what I needed. The cool air felt good on my hot cheeks. I had allowed myself to rant and cuss all the way over, sometimes under my breath and sometimes not. How could my mother accuse me of not trying? Why was she trying to force us into the perfect family model right away? Why couldn't she see that Daniel was just using us?

Entering the library, I told myself I wasn't going to think about Daniel anymore. He had taken up enough of my morning. I checked the new arrivals shelf and picked up a book that looked interesting. I found a couple more in the fiction section, then went to find a table.

On a whim, I went to the back table where I had sat with Robin. She was there again, sitting with Lia.

"Hi," I said, "mind if I join you?"

They looked up from their books and then glanced at each other. "Sure," Lia said, shrugging. "Why not?"

"If I'm not wanted, just say so," I said, stung that Robin hadn't immediately said yes. After all, I had included her in our group at lunch.

"We're working on a debate, Shadow," Robin said, "so that means no gossip."

"Me?" I put my hand dramatically to my chest. "I don't gossip. I never gossip."

"Whatever," she said.

Lia was a little friendlier. "We've just got a lot of work to do," she explained.

"So this is for an L-D debate?" I asked, pulling up my chair and moving some of their papers over.

"Shadow," Robin warned.

"What?"

"We're working."

"Maybe I can help. What's the resolution?"

"Shhh," said Robin. "You'll get us kicked out of the library."

Picking up a piece of paper, Lia quietly read, "Resolved: Capital punishment should be abolished." Robin went back to a book and started taking notes.

"Are you on the affirmative or negative?" I asked, keeping my voice down.

"Robin's affirmative," Lia said. "I'm negative."

"For the debate," Robin muttered.

Glancing at Robin, I asked, "Really? What about personally?"

"What do you mean?" Lia asked.

Robin groaned. "Shadow, we've got work to do!"

I ignored Robin and asked Lia, "Do you really believe that capital punishment should be abolished?"

"Absolutely," Lia said.

Robin put her book down. "You're kidding."

Lia looked surprised. "No. You don't agree?"

"I think capital punishment is a good idea," Robin said. "Especially for violent criminals who are repeat offenders."

"But killing is wrong."

"Not when someone deserves it."

"Hey, you guys," I said, glancing around. "Better keep it down."

"Who are you to judge who deserves it?" Lia demanded, ignoring me.

"I'm not," Robin said. "That's what the judge and jury are for."

"Who are they to decide? The only one who should have that right to decide is God."

"Then why did the murderer get to decide someone else should die?" Robin countered.

"I'm not saying the murderer shouldn't get punished, but they don't have to die. They deserve a second chance."

"Tell that to the person who was murdered!" Robin retorted.

Lia turned to me. "What do you think, Shadow?"

"Whoa, slow down here," I said, holding my hands up. "I was just asking a question. Besides, you'll have to argue both sides anyway."

"Yeah," said Lia. "Mr. Souza says that the best debaters know both sides of their argument, and that's why they're always ready with the rebuttals."

Robin looked at Lia. "He's right. Maybe that's how we can prepare. We'll debate each other first, so we'll know both sides of the issue."

"Let's get some more notes taken first. Then we can argue and see what angles we missed."

"Debate," Robin said. "We'll debate. We're not supposed to argue."

"What's the difference, anyway?" Lia asked.

"You get emotional in an argument," Robin began.

"And when you argue there aren't any rules," I added. "In a debate, you're limited on time and topics."

They went back to their notes and I skimmed through the books I had picked up, trying to decide which ones to check out.

After a few minutes, Lia turned to me. "You never did answer the question."

"What question?"

"Do you believe in capital punishment?"

"I don't know," I said.

"That's not an answer," Robin said.

I shrugged.

"We told you what we think."

"I really don't have an opinion," I said.

Robin and Lia both shook their heads and then went back to their books.

They didn't believe me, but it was true. I used to just assume that the death penalty was necessary. If you decided to kill someone else, you should give up your right to live too. But now, I wasn't so sure.

After about an hour, Robin and Lia left to go practice their debate at Lia's house. As I checked out the two books I had chosen, I looked over toward the computer banks in the back of the reference room.

On impulse, I did a search for the Denver paper. It took several minutes and a lot of backtracking to finally find the archived article.

Chapter Seven

It was just a tiny article buried in the back of the regional news section.

Local Man Charged with Murder

Daniel Thompson, 22, was arrested in connection with last month's murder of Reggie DiGallo. DiGallo was found dead in the Landon Arms Apartments on the 24th. Authorities had no comment on details of the case. A $250,000 bail has been set.

Two hundred fifty thousand dollars! And that didn't even count the lawyers' fees. No wonder Mom was worried about the finances. There was no way my parents had that much money.

Although finding the article didn't make me feel any better, at least I knew a little more. Wondering how the bail system worked, I did another search. I finally found a site that had the information I was looking for. It said that usually only 10 percent of the bail was needed to bond someone out of jail. But still, twenty-five thousand was a lot for my family. And if Daniel skipped out, we'd have to pay the entire amount.

I left the library, deep in thought. It was hard for me to believe that my brother could have killed someone. But if he wasn't guilty, why did he refuse to talk about what happened?

The skies looked heavy and I knew it would probably start raining soon. I didn't want to go home yet, so I stopped at the corner store and wandered up and down the aisles. The man at the counter started eyeing me like I was a shoplifter or something, so I bought a twenty-ounce Coke and a candy bar and left.

Just as I turned onto our street, I saw my mother's car back out of the driveway and head toward the mall. Relieved, I walked home quickly, hoping to beat the rain. There was a note waiting on the counter, for both Dad and me. It simply said Mom and Daniel would be back from shopping in time for dinner at 5:30, and since we would be home first, dinner was our job.

Great, I thought, and propped the note back up so Dad would see it when he came in.

As I walked down the hall, I felt a strong breeze. Daniel's bedroom door was open. Thunder cracked outside. I put the Coke and candy bar on my desk, tossed the books onto my bed, and then went into Daniel's room. The window was wide open, and the first raindrops were splattering on the windowsill.

I slid the window shut, and then hesitated as I turned to leave. For the last seven years, this room had felt strange, like it was waiting for someone. Now it seemed strange because there was someone staying in it. I looked around, feeling like I was trespassing.

The bed was neatly made and the clutter on the stereo was gone. The closet door was open, showing off its empty hangers and bare floor. It looked like a hotel room.

As I walked by the dresser, I glanced down. A CD case was on top of his otherwise immaculate dresser. I picked it up, wondering which musician Daniel found worth keeping. There wasn't a cover or CD in the case. Instead, there were photographs. *What a weird place to keep pictures,* I thought. I opened the case and took them out. The one on top was of Daniel with a girl. The other two were pictures of the same girl. She was pretty, although her smile seemed shy.

"Hello? Anyone home?" The garage door slammed shut.

I shoved the photos back in the jewel case and hurried out of Daniel's room. I managed to make it look like I was coming out of my room when Dad turned the corner in the hallway. He started a little bit.

"You could have at least answered," he said.

"Sorry."

"Where's everybody else?"

"Mom took Daniel shopping."

Chapter Seven

"Why didn't you go with them?"

"I needed to go to the library. Some of us were doing research for forensics."

He frowned. "I'm glad you're so excited about forensics," he said, "but I hope it won't interfere with your class work."

"It won't," I said. "I finished my homework this morning."

"Good," he said, nodding. Then he asked, "Did your mom say when they'd be back?"

"There's a note for us on the counter. It says we're in charge of dinner tonight."

He looked at me for a second, and then together we said, "Pizza."

He laughed. "We can order it later. I've got to check my e-mail."

In my room, I had to turn the light on because it had gotten so dark outside. The wind had really picked up too. After twenty minutes, the power went off. Dad and I went out on the porch and watched the storm together for a while. When we went back into the house, it was really dark. Dad found some candles and lit them. We tried ordering the pizza but the phone lines were down too. At about five minutes to six, Mom and Daniel came in.

"Sorry we're late," Mom said, kissing Dad on the cheek.

Daniel was right behind her, carrying two pizzas. "When we heard on the radio the power was out on this side of town, we decided we should stop."

So we had a candlelit pizza dinner. It was the most relaxed meal we ate all week. Mom and Daniel described the hard time they had getting out of the parking lot at the mall. The traffic lights were out and cars were backed up for blocks. That launched Dad into his story about canoeing down the main street during a flood when he was a kid, a story I'd heard every time it rained for more than an hour.

I kept waiting for Mom to say something about me walking out that morning, but she never did.

The power finally came back on a little after nine. We turned on the news and watched the footage of the storm damage. Several big trees had blown over not far from our neighborhood.

After the news, I said good night. I had just settled in with a book when there was a knock at the door.

"Yeah," I called.

"Mind if I come in for a minute?" Daniel asked, sticking his head in the door.

I shook my head and set my book aside. He sat down at my desk and peered into my backpack. He pulled out my chemistry book.

"How do you like chemistry?"

"It's a class," I said, not sure where this conversation might go. "It's not as boring as some."

"Is it your favorite?"

Shrugging, I said, "Yeah, I guess it is right now."

He was thinking. "I didn't have chemistry. I had some other science class."

"Earth science?"

"Yeah, that was it."

We were quiet for a few seconds.

"I don't see the money in here," he said, opening the front pocket of my backpack. "I wonder where it went."

I didn't take the bait. He had given me the money—forced it on me, really—so what I did with it was none of his business. But if he knew I gave it back, why didn't he just say so?

He pulled a roll of bills out of his pocket. "If I were as loaded or stoned as some of my old buddies, I probably never would have noticed."

I picked up my book again.

"You don't like money?"

"I like money just fine. I don't like not knowing where it came from."

Chapter Seven

"It came from me."

"But I don't know where you got it. I don't want any of your money and I don't want to know what you did to get it."

Daniel leaned forward. "I think you do want to know how I got it. You're dying to know. You're just afraid of the answer."

"Yeah," I said, meeting his stare. "You're right."

I could tell I had surprised him, admitting it like that. But then he sat up with a grin. "You're okay, Shadow. You still call it like you see it, just like you always did. Let me tell you where I got this money, so you can take it with a clean conscience. It's not drug money."

I was proud that I didn't blink. I kept my face straight, even though I had been sure that the only way he could make that much money that fast was with drugs. "I sold drugs for a while. I got out of it almost two years ago. You make quick bucks, but the risks are too high. I switched to hustling pool."

"You can make that much money playing pool?" I asked. I had no idea.

"No, man," Daniel closed his eyes and shook his head a little. "You make money on the books. I get a little pile of money going from the hustling, and then I play the books."

"What do you mean?"

"Betting? Bookies? The track, football, basketball, you name it, you can bet on it."

"I thought you'd been at the bar, not at the track."

"It's called off-track betting."

"Oh."

We were quiet again.

"Do you use drugs?" I asked.

"Not any more."

"Honestly?"

He snorted. "Why should I lie about using drugs? That's nothing compared to—" He broke off suddenly. "So, can I put it back

103

here?" he asked, opening my backpack pocket.

"No. I don't want it." I almost told him about my encounter with Mr. Morse, but something stopped me. I wanted to believe he was being truthful, but I didn't quite trust him.

"It really is yours. I owe you."

"I don't want your money."

"You're the first," he mumbled.

"What?"

"Shad, everyone on the streets wants something from you, and it almost always comes down to cash. And if you don't pay your debts with cash, you pay with something else."

Like what? I wanted to ask. When Daniel picked up a couple of my CD's, I blurted out, "So who's the girl?"

He glanced behind him. "What girl?"

"The one in the pictures on your dresser."

"What were you doing snooping around my stuff?" His tone sounded just like it did when I was little and I had gone into his room without permission.

"You left the window open during the storm. I went in to shut it. Next time I'll just let your room flood."

He seemed to relax. A little.

"So, who is she?"

He started to walk away. "Her name's Robin."

"You're joking!"

He whipped around and stared at me. "Do I look like I'm joking?"

"I just—" The look in his eyes scared me. "Never mind. So, is she your girlfriend?"

He opened the door. "It's late. I'm sure you want to get back to your book. Good night." He shut the door behind him.

Chapter Eight

On Sunday, Mom decided we would take a family trip to the museum. I looked at Dad, waiting for him to object or come up with an excuse, but he merely continued eating his cereal. I still wasn't worried though; I was sure Daniel would be as thrilled about going to a museum as I was. Besides, there was also the chance he wouldn't even wake up before it closed.

It was shocking, then, to find myself in the backseat of the car before ten. Not only had Daniel not objected to the plan, he'd expanded on it: "That sounds great! Why don't we go to the zoo first? Before it gets too hot."

I tried not to stare at Daniel too much. I was having a hard time matching what he had told me last night with his behavior today; it simply wasn't lining up. At first I was really on edge, waiting until Daniel said something to spoil the mood, but as the day went on, I began to relax. We spent the day doing things I never thought we'd do again—wandering the zoo together for two hours in the morning, eating a leisurely hour and a half lunch, and touring the museum all afternoon. I didn't think anyone was acting; we all seemed to be enjoying each other's company. On the ride home, I could especially tell how happy Mom was. I silently apologized to her for my earlier doubts. I had had a good time.

I went in to do some reading when we got home. When I came out of my room, I was surprised to find Daniel in the kitchen, helping Mom fix dinner.

"Anything I can do to help?" I asked.

"You could set the table," Mom suggested.

As I put out the plates and silverware, I could hear them talking and laughing together. After I finished with the table, I asked if there was anything else I could do. They didn't hear me. They were too busy discussing the recipe. Ignoring the hollowness in my stomach, I left the kitchen.

Dad was in the living room reading the newspaper. He smiled up at me as I came in and sat down, but didn't say anything. I wondered if he was feeling left out too.

Everything went fine at dinner. Just as we were finishing the dishes, Dad spoke up. "So, Dan, what are your plans for tomorrow?" he asked.

My brother shrugged. "I hadn't given it much thought," he said, turning to Mom. "Can I borrow your car tomorrow?"

Dad didn't move, but I could almost feel him tense up.

Mom hesitated, and then shook her head. "I really need the car tomorrow and Tuesday. Maybe on Wednesday, but we'll have to see."

It seemed to me that the tension drained out of Dad and went directly to Daniel.

"Well," Dad said, sounding casual, "if you don't have anything planned for tomorrow, you could mow the lawn."

That was my job, but if Dad wanted Daniel to do it, why should I care?

"Sure," Daniel said. "If I have time." He reached in the refrigerator and got a beer.

"Never mind," Dad said. "I'll do it when I get home from work." The nice feeling from this morning and afternoon had disappeared.

Chapter Eight

I escaped out the back door and sat on the steps. I had only been there a few minutes when Daniel came out and sat down beside me.

"Hey," he said.

"Hey."

"I get the feeling Dad's not real happy."

"Glad you could pick up on that," I said.

Daniel shot me a look. I didn't care. We had had a good weekend, and it was his fault that everything was falling apart again.

"Well, there's nothing I can do about it now," he said.

"You could mow the lawn before he gets home tomorrow," I pointed out. "And if that's too much, why don't you try getting home on time?"

"Thanks for the tip." He folded his arms across his knees and put his head down.

"What's wrong?" I asked.

"You mean other than being accused of murder? I don't know. Haven't really had time to think about much else."

"You act like it's the end of the world."

"Isn't it?" he asked. Before I could respond, he continued, "No. You're right. It's not the end of the world. It's just the end of my freedom."

"I thought—"

"Unless I get the chair," Daniel continued. "Then it's the end of my life."

"But Mom said that lawyer is—"

"Shadow, it looks bad, okay? Even if I plead not guilty, no one's gonna believe an ex–drug-dealing, pool-hustling punk like me." He stood up. "Guess I'll see you tomorrow afternoon," he said.

"Daniel?"

"It's Dan," he said, turning around.

"Why did you leave?" I managed to keep my voice steady.

Running a hand through his hair, he sighed. "You know, it's

stupid, 'cause I don't even remember. I never intended to stay away so long, though. I remember thinking I'd stay away for a week, just to show them. Then the week became a month, and six months went by. After a while it was just too late to come home."

"It was never too late, Daniel."

He gave me a weak grin. "I didn't know that."

"Where did you stay?" I pressed. "What did you do?"

"You don't want to know."

"I wouldn't ask if I didn't want to know."

Daniel looked at me for a long moment before he shook his head. "Maybe if I don't tell you, I can feel like I've done something to protect my little brother. Good night, Shad." He opened the back door.

"Dan, Mom and Dad have done a lot for you in the last week," I said quietly. "They would have done it every day of your life if you hadn't run away. Think about it."

In spite of Sunday night, the week seemed to start pretty well. I don't know what Dan was doing to pass the time, but he was home every day by the time I got there. When Mom apologetically told him that she still needed the car on Wednesday and Thursday, he didn't get an attitude about it.

School was fine. I only saw Mr. Barnett in the hall once, and he was so busy chewing out someone else that he didn't even notice me. I went to Vernon's after school on Monday, and on Tuesday we stayed at school to practice a Lincoln-Douglas debate. I was disappointed that Robin didn't join us after school, but she promised to be there for regular practice the next day.

Vernon and I were in room 28 by 3:02 on Wednesday. Lia and Erica were already there. Ryan showed up next, and told us that Russ had gone home sick and wouldn't be coming. Several people

I didn't know came in and started going through file cabinets. Pat walked in with another upperclassman, and around ten after, Tess made her entrance. She gave Pat a quick kiss.

Vernon nudged me with his elbow. "Looks like you waited too long," he whispered.

"I told you she had a boyfriend," I whispered back.

Together, Pat and Tess began to explain the interpretive speeches. There were several different kinds, but they all basically fell into two categories: speeches you memorized and prepared ahead of time, and speeches on topics that were given to you five minutes before you presented them.

Pat was in the middle of explaining "The Interpretation of Humorous Literature" when Robin walked in. He stopped talking and gave her a dirty look as she looked for a place to sit.

"Hey, Robin," I called out. "Over here! We saved a seat for you." For my trouble, all I got was a dirty look from both Pat *and* Robin. She sat down four desks away.

Tess and Pat took another fifteen minutes explaining the different events. Then Tess told us to break up into two groups. "Those of you who think you'd like to try the interpretive readings go to the right side of the room," she instructed, "and those of you who want to do the impromptu events go to the left. You'll get the chance to try the other events later if you want to. This is just to get started."

Vernon turned to me. "What are you going to do?"

"I don't know," I said, glancing at Robin. She moved over two desks, to the left side of the room.

"I think the impromptu stuff sounds fun," I said. Getting a topic and only having five or ten minutes to prepare it did sound more challenging than just reading something.

Vernon made a face. "I really think I'd do better at the readings," he said slowly.

"Okay, see you later," I said. I could tell he thought I was try-ing to get rid of him. "We can compare notes on the way home," I added.

Vernon picked up his bag and went to the right side of the room. Ryan went with him. Erica and Lia were discussing where to go. I got my stuff and moved over next to Robin.

"Sorry," I said.

She didn't look at me.

"I was trying to help."

"You thought embarrassing me would help?"

I winced. "I wasn't trying to embarrass you. I was trying to get Pat's attention away from you."

"By calling my name in the middle of what he was saying?"

"I said I was sorry."

"You should be."

"Do you accept my apology?"

She looked at me out of the corner of her eye. "I'll think about it."

By now Erica and Lia and one other sophomore, a guy named Paul, had seated themselves by us, and everyone else was on the other side of the room. Pat and Tess picked up some papers, and I tried not to groan when Pat came over to our group.

"We'll try to get two kinds of speeches done today," he said. "The first one is Creative Storytelling. I'm going to give each of you a piece of paper with characters, setting, and a situation writ-ten on it. You'll have fifteen minutes to prepare. You can write ideas down, but you can't use any notes during the presentation." He started passing out half-sheets of paper. "Um, this is going to be a little different from a meet, because in a meet situation you're given three story outlines to choose from, and you have to stay within the time limit. Today, since we're all going to listen to each other's stories, you'll only be given one story option, not three. And those of you who go last will actually have a little longer than fifteen minutes. Any questions?"

Chapter Eight

"How long should our story be?" I asked.

He gave me a killer glare, and I could tell he thought I was trying to piss him off. I really wasn't. He hadn't said anything about the length of the stories.

"Between three and five minutes. Any other questions?" His stare dared me to ask one, but I was ready to get this over with.

"Good," he said. "Your fifteen minutes start now."

My paper said:

Characters: Princess, Prince
Setting: Castle in Ireland
Situation: The Princess's mom is coming to visit

Are the topics all this stupid? I wondered. *Or did Pat give me this one on purpose?* Maybe he was trying to make a point with me. I tried to glance at Paul's and Robin's papers, but they were both bent over their desks, already writing away. I pulled out a blank piece of paper and started scribbling. After a minute, I felt someone staring at me. I glanced up, right into Robin's brown eyes. She immediately looked down at her paper, blushing.

"What?"

"Nothing."

"What?" I demanded.

"Nothing!" She glared at me.

"Fine." I shrugged and went back to work. Every once in a while, I thought I could feel her eyes on me, but I never caught her looking at me again.

"Time's up," Pat said.

I wasn't the only one who groaned as I put my pen down. I had barely gotten my story completed. I hadn't even had time to run through it once.

"I'll need your papers before you speak, so I can check that you did the right story and write my comments."

I picked up my pen to change part of what I had written. Pat cleared his throat loudly. I sat back in my chair, but I didn't put my pen down.

"So who wants to go first?"

We all shifted uncomfortably in our chairs.

Pat paused for a few seconds and then smiled. "How about you, Shadowman? Why don't you start us off?"

I swallowed hard and stood up. There was no point in arguing. It was only a practice run, but I still felt almost physically ill. I had been telling myself that this really wasn't a speech, that I could handle talking in front of our team. But I was wrong. As soon as I turned to face the others, the last drop of saliva in my mouth evaporated. I have never wanted so badly to run away.

I cleared my throat twice. I glanced nervously at the other side of the room, but they were all discussing their readings and not paying any attention to us.

"Sometime today," Pat said.

Not even being pissed at him could get me over my fear. I cleared my throat again, praying that my voice wouldn't crack on me. Then I began.

"Once upon a time, a long time in the future, a princess and prince were living in their castle in Ireland." There, I had stated almost all of my required subjects. Quickly I added, "Princess Lori was getting excited about her mother's visit. She was coming all the way from the planet Zitzoid."

I saw Paul whisper something to Lia.

"Prince Jim, however, wasn't too crazy about having his mother-in-law to visit. He wanted to go star-surfing instead. He begged and pleaded with the princess, but she said if he didn't stay for the visit, she would cancel his membership with the Cha-Tet." I could see the confusion on the faces in my audience.

"Um...the Cha-Tet was the elite star-surfing club. Only the

best star-surfers could join." I still had my pen in my hand and I began twirling it between my fingers.

"'When will she be here?' Prince Jim asked.

"'She can beam over here tonight,' the princess replied. 'Maybe we could all go surfing together.'

"'Why would we want to do that?'

"'Because she'll pay for everything.'

My voice squeaked on the last word. I took a deep breath and tried to slow down. I was going too fast and knew there was no way my story would last for three minutes.

"'Your mother couldn't surf a star if she held it with all of her hands,' the prince said. 'How long will she be staying anyway? She'd better be gone before the championships.'

"'My mother can stay as long as she wants to. After all, she gave us the Xanium to fill the moat. You always say the Xanium makes you the best star-surfer.'"

I paused in hopes of a laugh or a giggle or some kind of response. Nothing. I was dying.

Desperately, I tried to move my story along.

"The mother-in-law was more like a mother to the prince than his own mother, but he still didn't want to spend any time with her." I switched the pen to my left hand and kept twirling it. "Princess Lori knew why her mother was coming to visit, but she didn't want to tell the prince yet." My voice cracked again. Pat snorted. "It was supposed to be a big surprise."

I was so rattled, I couldn't even remember my character's names. "That night, the mother-in-law beamed over in her convertible space rocket.

"The prince was just about to slip out the back door of the castle when the princess stopped him. 'Wait,' she said. 'Mother has something for you. An early birthday present.'"

Suddenly, the pen flipped out of my hand and bounced off the desk, clattering to the floor. At least Erica and Lia were smiling now. I didn't dare glance at Robin.

I couldn't stand much more of this. I had to finish quickly. I didn't care how short the story was.

"The prince couldn't believe his eyes. His mother-in-law was holding in her hands a brand-new, state-of-the-art Asteroidian Star-Surfboard!

"'This is great!' said the prince. 'Simply stellar! I'll be sure to win the star-surfing championship now!'"

I practically dove into my seat, leaving my pen on the floor.

"You're not allowed to use props, especially flying pens," Pat said as he made a couple of notes.

Everyone giggled.

"You didn't say anything about props when you gave us directions," Lia said.

Pat glared at her. "Okay. Anybody have any comments?"

"I thought it was good for a first try," Lia said.

No one else said anything. They were all staring down at their papers. I suddenly realized that most of them had probably been paying more attention to their own notes than to what I had been saying.

"Let's see," Pat said, scanning his critique sheet. "That was kind of short. And it didn't make a whole lot of sense. You should have explained what star-surfing and Xanium were. But you did use all of your elements. Another thing—you need to slow down. You were really rushing at the end."

"I just wanted to sit down," I mumbled.

He ignored me and continued, "You need to look at your audience. Eye contact counts." Pat checked his notes again. "Your ending was really weak."

"That's because I changed it as I went."

Pat shook his head. "That's never a good idea. How many times did you run through it before you got up there?"

"I didn't."

He nodded smugly. "You need to be able to create the story and practice it at least three times in the fifteen-minute prep time," he said. "That's the big thing, making it within the time limits. If you go over or under, they automatically rank you fourth or last." He put down the sheet and looked around the group. "Who wants to go next?"

I was the only one not trying to melt into my chair, because I had already gone. Pat waited a little longer this time for a volunteer before choosing Robin.

She handed him her outline and gave me an unreadable look before starting her story. I guess she figured Pat wouldn't have known her name if I hadn't called it out when she came in.

Her voice started off a little too soft and quiet, but as she went along, it got stronger. Her story was a cute one about a dragon stuck in a damp cave who couldn't remember how to breathe fire.

She sat down.

"Good job," Erica said.

"That was really good," Paul said. "I could almost picture that dragon."

"Nicely done," Pat agreed, finishing his notes. "It was three minutes, forty-five seconds. You used all of your elements, and you didn't rush too badly. Your eye contact wasn't bad, either. You do need to work a little on your volume, though, because you were hard to hear at the beginning. Okay, who wants to go next?"

Erica, Lia, and then Paul all did their stories. Robin's was the best one by far.

Pat stood up. "Well, it's almost four-thirty, so there's not enough time to try another type of speech. We'd better stop now. Don't forget, the story outlines are found in the filing cabinet, if you want to practice them from time to time. There's also a file with impromptu topics, so you can practice those. Of course, for the impromptu speeches, you only get five minutes to prepare, but you can use note cards while you give the speech." He gave us the critique sheets he had filled out for each of our stories.

Vernon's group was still working. Robin picked up her bag and walked out the door. I looked over at Vernon, hesitated for a moment, and then went after Robin. I had to run to catch her.

"Hey, Robin!" I called.

She glanced over her shoulder and slowed down a little, but she didn't stop. She was heading toward the door on the opposite side of the building from the one I normally used.

I caught up with her just as she stepped out of the building. "I guess this means I'm not forgiven," I panted.

"I still haven't decided."

"Your story was great."

"Kissing up is not going to get you forgiven."

"No, I mean it! Your story was the best. Mine stunk."

"I wouldn't say it stunk…" she began.

"But you certainly can't say it was good." I finished her sentence for her.

"You looked really nervous."

"I was," I said. "And if I was that nervous just for our teammates, how am I going to be in front of strangers? Maybe I should try the impromptu stuff, so I can have a note card to stare at instead." We came to the first corner and turned left.

"The eye contact is what kills me," I continued. "I can't handle looking at people when they aren't responding to what I'm saying."

"So don't look at them."

"Then I don't get the good marks," I said, holding up the critique sheet Pat had filled out.

"I don't look at people," she said.

"You did today."

"No, I looked *through* them. It's a trick I learned from my dad. He has to do a lot of public speaking. I let my eyes move around the room, but I'm not really focusing on anyone. It's hard to explain," she said, noticing my confused look. "You kind of let your eyes fuzz over, so it looks like you're making eye contact, but you don't really see anyone."

"I think I understand," I said slowly. "I'll have to try it next time. Thanks."

She nodded her head a little. We walked on quietly for a few minutes, turning another corner.

"I didn't know you lived over here," she said finally.

"I don't."

Robin stopped and stared at me. "Then why are you walking this way?" she demanded.

"I wanted to talk to you. You wouldn't stop walking, so I just walked with you."

"So where do you live?"

I pointed back in the direction we had come from.

"You walked all this way just to talk to me? Why?"

I started to answer and then stopped. Ahead, just past the next street corner, I could see a big sign.

"Want to go get a burger?" I asked.

She looked at her watch. "Okay. Sure."

We walked over to the fast food place, and I bought us each a burger, large fries, and a Coke. We sat down in a booth in the back. At first Robin did most of the talking, but then she started asking me questions. Before I knew it, I was telling her about some of my failed sports attempts, making her laugh. We were both having fun. Suddenly, we realized that the sun was almost down.

"I'd better get going," Robin said.

"Yeah," I said. "I didn't realize it was this late."

We left the restaurant and walked back the way we came. She tried to tell me to go home when we got back to the corner.

"I'll walk you home first."

"You don't have to do that," she said.

"Sure I do."

"What if I don't want you to know where I live?"

"Look, I'm not going to let you walk home alone. Either we walk together or I walk fifteen feet behind you, but either way I'm going to make sure you get home okay."

She laughed. "You're really sweet, you know that?"

"Don't tell anyone," I said, flipping up the collar of my leather jacket and hunching down a little. "I don't want to wreck the terrifying reputation that I worked so hard to get."

She laughed again. "You? Terrifying? I don't think so."

I walked her the rest of the way home. When we got there, I resisted the urge to ask to use her phone. I could be home in fifteen minutes if I walked fast.

"Thanks for the burger," she said.

"No problem," I said, shifting from one foot to the other. She looked over her shoulder at the door. I thought I saw someone move behind the glass. "I guess I'll see you tomorrow."

"Yeah," she said. "At lunch."

I turned and walked down the driveway.

"Oh, Shadow?"

"Yeah?" I swung back around.

She was standing in the door. "You're forgiven."

I grinned. "Thanks."

I tried to jog home, but I wasn't used to running and my backpack bounced awkwardly against my shoulder. It was nearly six-thirty when I walked in the front door.

"Where have you been?" Mom demanded before I even had the door shut. She jumped out of her seat and hurried toward me. Dad and Daniel were in their regular places in the living room.

"I had forensics practice today. I told you that."

She got up in my face. "Don't lie to me!" she nearly shouted.

Chapter Eight

"I'm not lying!"

"Where were you?" She was shaking.

I began again. "Forensics practice—"

"Vernon called here almost two hours ago, looking for you," she cut in. "Forensics practice ended at four!"

"Four-thirty," I corrected.

Mom slapped me, hard across the face.

Absolute silence descended. I slowly raised my hand. Mom was pale and there were tears glistening in her eyes as she took a half step back.

"Shadow." Dad's quiet voice had steel behind it.

Until Dad spoke, I wasn't really aware of what my hand was doing. It was kind of a shock to realize I had been ready to slap Mom back. Instead, I touched my cheek, then simply walked out of the living room, down the hall and into my room, slamming the door behind me.

My parents rarely ever raised their voices to me, and neither of them had ever hit me before.

I threw my backpack over by my desk. I was too angry to sit down. I paced back and forth in my cramped room, my long strides making it almost seem like I was just spinning around. Finally I drew a deep breath, and then another. I sank down into the chair and picked up the phone.

There was a knock at the door.

"I'm on the phone!"

The door opened anyway.

"I said I'm on the phone!"

Dad came in, followed by Mom. "We need to talk, Shadow," he said.

"I have nothing to say."

"Put the phone down."

I glared at him, and he calmly met my eyes. Mom wasn't looking at me. I slammed the phone down and stood up.

"Thank you. I'm sorry to be interrupting your call, but we need to talk before this gets out of hand."

"Mom seems to have everything in her hand," I said bitterly.

She looked up at me. Tears were streaming down her face. "Shadow." Her voice broke. "Shadow, I'm sorry. I'm so sorry." She dissolved into quiet sobs.

Dad waited for me to say something, but when I didn't, he put his arm around her. "Your mother was extremely upset."

"So that makes it okay?"

"I'm trying to explain this to you," Dad said, a bit sharply. He took a deep breath. "You know you're supposed to call if you're going to be late. We had no idea where you were or if you were okay."

"I just lost track of time."

"You know how important it is for us to know where you are," he said.

"If I were going to run away, you should know I'd be nice like Daniel and leave you a note," I said.

Mom's sobs got louder. She covered her face with both hands and stumbled out of the room. I felt less than an inch tall, but I was still pissed. I was late for the second time in seven years and I got slapped for it, before I even got a chance to explain where I was. It wasn't fair.

Dad turned and looked at me, anger evident in his face. "You will apologize to her for that last remark."

I simply nodded as I sank back down into my chair.

"What happened this afternoon?"

Stubbornly, I didn't answer.

"Shadow, I don't like this change in attitude." I had to admire Dad. His face was all tense and red, but his voice was as calm as ever. "You've always been such a good kid—"

"Yeah, and instead of being trusted because of it, I get punished the instant I make one tiny mistake!"

Chapter Eight

Sighing, he sat down on my bed. "I know this isn't going to help much, but you just picked the wrong day to lose track of time."

"What do you mean?"

"Your brother came in, oh, maybe fifteen minutes ago."

"So we were both late. Did she slap him too?"

He glared at me.

"Sorry," I muttered, stubbing the toe of my shoe into the carpet.

"His shirt was torn and dirty, and he's got a black eye."

"What happened?"

"He won't tell us. Mom was worried about both of you, but when he walked in hurt like that... Well, her nerves have been stretched pretty tight anyway. So you walked in, she saw you were okay, and it was like everything snapped."

"Across my face."

"If you don't quit making those comments, you're going to get slapped again!"

I stared at the desk. Dad took another deep breath.

"It was your smart-aleck tone that earned you the slap."

"I wasn't being a smart aleck," I protested.

"It's your tone of voice, Shadow," he cut in. "And you're doing it again."

"Sorry," I said, thinking that I needed to tape record my voice so I could start figuring out which tone was the smart-aleck one. Lately it seemed to come out a lot more than I intended.

"So where were you this afternoon?"

I shrugged. "I walked a girl home after practice, and we stopped for a burger, okay? We were talking so much, we didn't realize how late it was."

He just looked at me, but I could tell he was trying to decide my level of honesty. I'm glad he didn't question it out loud though; I wasn't sure what my response would have been.

"Can I make my call now?" I asked.

"Dinner will be ready in a few minutes," he said, standing up.

"So make your phone call quick."

"Right."

He tried to grin. "So is she cute?"

I rolled my eyes at him. "Dad," I moaned.

He looked at me like he wanted to say something else, or maybe he was expecting me to say something, but then he just stood up and left. Part of me wanted to crawl into bed and wait until everything sorted itself out. The other part of me wanted to grab everyone in a huge hug and hold them there until we could all talk like rational human beings.

Instead, I picked up the phone again and called Vernon.

"Hello?"

"Hey, Vern," I said.

"Thanks for ditching me, man."

"Sorry," I said. "Your group was still talking."

"You could have waited for me."

"I know, I know."

"So where'd you go?" he asked.

"I walked Robin home."

He started laughing. "Boy, you don't waste any time. Find out one girl's taken and you just move on to the next."

I didn't say anything. It would be pointless to remind him I'd never said I was interested in Tess.

"So are you two going out now?"

"I don't know. Ask her. Look, I've got to go eat. Have you done the trig yet?"

"Half of it. It's actually kind of tough tonight."

"Great," I said. "Maybe I'll call you later for some answers."

"Sure," he said, "I only charge a hundred dollars per answer, or for five hundred, you can get the correct one."

"You're weird, Vern," I said, hanging up. Hesitantly, I walked down the hall to the living room. Dad and Daniel were in their seats. If I hadn't known better, I would have said neither of them had moved since I came in. I could hear Mom clattering around in the kitchen.

I took a deep breath and stepped into the kitchen. "Smells good," I said. "Need any help?"

"No thanks," she said, clearing her throat. "I think everything's under control."

"Can I set the table?"

"Daniel already did."

"Oh." She wouldn't look at me, and it felt awkward. Finally I just blurted out, "I'm sorry, Mom."

She made a sad smile. "Me too, honey."

I felt like we should hug or something, but she stayed where she was, stirring something in the pan. Feeling a little empty, I went back out into the living room.

Needless to say, dinner that night was extremely uncomfortable. It was at least as bad as the first night Daniel had come home, if not worse. Mom had been carrying almost all of our meal conversations, and she hardly said a word. It was too bad we hadn't gone out for dinner, just to get a change of pace.

We finished dinner, and I practically leapt up. "I'll do the dishes," I said, grabbing the salad bowl.

"I'll help," Daniel said.

Together we cleared the table and put the dishes in the dishwasher. Mom and Dad went out to the living room. Daniel didn't say a word until we were putting the last glasses in the washer.

"Boy, Mom really freaked about you being late."

"She was freaked about both of us," I said. "What happened to you?"

He shrugged. "Just a fight. But I don't think she really even noticed that. She just…"

"Flipped out because you weren't home yet?"

"Exactly! What's the big deal about being a little late?"

"It's a big deal if you're afraid someone might never come home again."

"Oh. Guess I kind of screwed things up for you, huh?"

"Not just for me," I said. "For all of us."

"Maybe I should go stay somewhere else," he said.

I snorted. "You really hate us that much?"

"It would be easier—" he began, but the phone interrupted.

I picked it up as I followed Dan to the living room. "Hello?"

"Hi, this is Jan Moore from the *Denver Post*."

"Oh, we already get the—"

"No, no," she said quickly. "I'm not calling for sales. I'm a reporter. I'd like to arrange an interview with Daniel Thompson, or with someone else in the family. "

My mouth went dry.

"Are you his brother? Could I ask—"

I hung up.

"Who was that?" Dad asked.

I was staring at the phone. It rang again in my hand. "Hello."

"Hi, this is Jan Moore again. We must have been—"

I hung up the phone again, then set it on the table.

"Shadow?" Mom asked.

"What's going on?" Dad demanded.

"A reporter from the *Post*," I said.

"Damn it! Why won't they leave us alone?" Dad practically shouted. "If this keeps up, we're going to have to get an unlisted number." He picked up the handset and began fiddling with it.

"Mark," Mom pleaded.

"They've called before?" I asked, startled. "Why didn't you tell me?"

"We didn't want to upset you, honey," Mom said soothingly.

"Mom, you have to stop protecting me!" I looked at Daniel.

"Did you know about this?"

"Yeah. They called a couple of times during the day. Maclean said not to talk to the media, but I gave the reporter a few quotes before I hung up. Stuff they can't put in the paper."

"There," Dad said. "I've turned the ringer off for now. If they want to keep calling, they can just listen to our voice mail message."

I escaped to my room and worked on homework for almost an hour. I tried calling Vernon a couple of times, but his line was busy. I had just picked up my library book when I heard someone coming down the hall.

"Hey, Shadow. You still awake?"

It was Daniel.

"Yeah. Come in," I said.

"Hey," he said, opening the door.

"Hey. What's up?"

He shook his head. "It's not much fun out there."

"I'm glad it's not just me."

"So why were *you* late?"

"Lost track of time," I said.

He dropped down on the floor in the middle of my room. "I used to use that excuse. What were you doing to make you lose track of time?"

"Walking around with a friend," I said.

"Who? Someone from that speech team?"

"Yeah."

"Was it a girl?" His grin got a little devilish. He almost looked like the old Daniel I remembered.

"Yeah." I shifted uncomfortably.

"So what's she look like?"

"Brown hair, brown eyes."

"Cute?"

"Sort of."

"What's her name?"

"Robin."

He stiffened up. "That's not funny."

"I'm not joking."

Daniel stared at me. "You're serious?"

"Yeah."

"That's weird, man."

"I know."

We were both quiet for a minute.

"Where's your Robin now?" I asked. "You still talk to her?"

He shook his head but didn't answer. He didn't leave, though, and I took that for a good sign.

"So how'd you get the black eye?" I asked.

"At Rocker's," he said, cocking an eyebrow at me. "Where else?"

"So why didn't you just tell Mom and Dad about that?"

Shrugging, he said, "I don't think they'd want to hear all the dirty details."

"Maybe not all of them," I agreed. "But surely they'd like to know why you came in looking like that. Was the fight over a bet or your pool game?"

"My pool game." He pulled at a strand of carpet. "I don't want to tell Mom and Dad what's going on. I don't think I can stand to disappoint them any more than I already have."

"So don't. Quit going to the bar and—"

"Shadow, I know you're trying to help," he broke in, "but lay off, okay? I'm going to disappoint them again. There's no way to avoid it." He muttered to himself, "I never should have called that night."

I was searching for a response to that as he stood up. He turned around when he reached the door. "You asked about my Robin. I don't see her anymore. I can't. She's dead."

Chapter Nine

Having spent the last few days avoiding Daniel, I now found it frustrating that I couldn't find any time alone with him. I desperately wanted to ask him about his Robin, but was sure he wouldn't talk about it in front of Mom and Dad. He had to know I wanted to talk to him, but now it seemed that he was avoiding me.

Over the next week, I checked the on-line edition of the Denver paper every day, but I didn't see anything else about Daniel's case. Not a word was said in our house about lawyers or trials or my brother's dead girlfriend.

Daniel occasionally did small chores around the house during the day; usually he was asleep in his room when I got home from school. Sometimes he was up by the time Mom came in from work, but not often. He wasn't eating much, either, no matter what favorite dish Mom cooked for him. The new clothes she had bought him hung on him like he was no more than a wire hanger. Mom was disappointed when Daniel repeatedly refused her offers to fix up his room.

Although the tension between Mom and Dad seemed to have eased off, the tension between Mom and me had gotten worse. I had apologized for being late, and she had apologized for slapping me. There was still something between us, though, and I didn't know how to fix it. I wondered if that was how Daniel had felt all those years ago when he was fifteen. My conflict with Mom was nothing compared to some of the fights Daniel had had with Dad.

I remembered one time in particular. Daniel had plastered posters on his wall and replaced all of the lightbulbs in his room with black lights. Only six, I had been in awe of the way my shirt had looked in the eerie light. Dad hadn't paid much attention to our clothing, however, because he had been livid about the posters. I never really had much of a chance to look at them, because Dad had ripped them off the wall so fast. He ordered me out of the room, but the yelling started before I got through the door.

Looking back, I realized that other things must have been going on that I simply wasn't aware of.

On Saturday, I met Robin at the library. After we studied for a while, I walked her to her house. On the way, we passed through a park. Somehow, we ended up racing for the jungle gym.

"Can I ask you a personal question?"

I looked at her as she climbed past me. "You can ask, but I might not answer."

"Why do you always wear black?" She stopped just a little short of the top.

"Because," I whispered, trying to sound mysterious. "I'm really a vampire."

"Shadow—"

"To maintain my terrifying image," I said in my best Dracula accent.

"Never mind," she said in an exasperated tone just like my mother's. "Sorry I asked."

"I don't really have a reason." I managed a grin, but I felt embarrassed and self-conscious. I climbed to the triangle just below her. "I started a couple years ago, to be different, I guess. Now, it's more of a habit."

She had a gleam in her eye. "What would it take to get you to wear something besides black?"

"I don't know," I said. I had actually considered wearing another color several times, but the thought of the grief I would get the day I did had stopped me. I had trapped myself very neatly.

"Are you going to wear black to the meets?"

"Sure. I've got a real nice black silk button-down shirt."

She moved gracefully to the top, and looked down at me thoughtfully. "So you wear black everywhere you go? What if you were playing tennis?"

"I don't play tennis...or golf," I added, trying to stop her line of conversation.

"What about Homecoming?"

The Homecoming dance had been announced earlier this week. It was still almost a month away. "I've never gone to dances," I said slowly. "But if I did go..." I stopped to think for a moment, but then shook my head. "...I'd probably wear all black there too."

She slipped between the bars and swung, hand over hand, till she was back at my level.

"You part monkey?"

Robin laughed as she pulled herself up through the bars. "I loved hanging around the jungle gym when I was in elementary school."

"Obviously," I said, and she gave me a light swat on the shoulder. "Okay, my turn for a question."

She gave me a measuring look. "You can ask, but I might not answer."

"You told me you were doing debate for your career, but you never would tell me what you want to do. Will you tell me now?"

She shrugged. "It's really no big deal," she said.

"That's avoiding the question," I said.

"I didn't promise to answer it," she responded.

"Tell me this: Was one of my guesses right?"

Flushing, she nodded.

"Well, then I'm sorry for whatever insult I added to your chosen career."

She smiled at me and then jumped lightly off her perch. I followed with a little less grace.

"When are you and Lia debating the death penalty?"

"Wednesday."

"Are you ready?"

"I think so. We've got our arguments outlined, and we've done a practice run at home. It's been hard, though, because Lia is really against the death penalty, and she can get a little emotional about it."

"And you still believe in it?"

"Yeah. It's kind of personal for me. Four years ago, my dad's cousin and his wife were murdered."

"Wow. I'm sorry."

"They lived in Los Angeles, and we didn't see them a whole lot. The police caught the guy who did it. But even though he was convicted and sentenced to life in prison, he could be out on parole in only eight more years."

I frowned.

"It just makes me mad, you know?" Robin continued. "I mean, this jerk not only took two lives, but he devastated my grandparents and aunts and uncles, and all he has to do is sit in a cell and get fed three meals a day. He's even got cable and access to a gym! And do you know why he did it?"

I wasn't sure I wanted to know, but it was a rhetorical question.

"He needed money for drugs. He broke into their house, started stealing stuff to sell, and when they walked in on him, he just killed them. Because they were in the way," she said bitterly.

"They had the nerve to walk into their own home and he killed them."

There was nothing I could say.

After a few moments, she said, "You never did tell us which side you were on. Are you for it or against it? How would you feel if someone in your family had been murdered?"

"Wait. I bet I know," I said, determined to change the conversation. "You joined debate to practice being a lawyer."

"Now who's avoiding the question?" she teased.

"Let me guess. You want to be a prosecutor."

She nodded, looking a little self-conscious.

"You're going to put the scum of the earth away for life."

"Okay, okay. You've made your point," she said, laughing. Then she looked at me carefully. "Now back to my question. Are you for the death penalty?"

"I used to be for it," I said, after hesitating for a second. "But now I'm not so sure."

"What do you mean?"

"It's personal for me too."

"How so?"

Briefly, I told her about Daniel.

When I finished, Robin was shaking her head. "I can't believe you let me go on about the death penalty like that. Why didn't you just tell me to shut up? I don't know what I'd be feeling if I were you."

"I've spent the last couple of weeks trying to figure out how I feel."

"Have you been able to talk with your brother?"

"Not really. It's hard, because I really don't know him. He's not like he used to be. At least not like I remembered him." I tried not to think of Daniel's comment about his Robin, the flat tone of his voice when he told me that she was dead.

"Do you think he killed someone?"

131

"I don't know."

She looked at me carefully. "Yes, you do. You have an opinion."

She was right. I did know what I thought. I just couldn't bring myself to say it out loud. "I don't know," I repeated stubbornly.

"You know, what you said before about me putting all the scum of the earth away for life? That doesn't necessarily mean your brother."

"I know," I said, but I wasn't convinced.

"Has he told you anything about what happened?"

"No." The brief newspaper article flashed through my mind. "That's what makes it so hard. He never wants to talk about it."

"Maybe he did it, but it was self-defense. Or maybe it was an accident."

"Maybe," I said.

Conversation kind of dragged after that. I walked her home again, even though she kept protesting that it was too far out of my way.

Right before she disappeared into the house, she suddenly said, "Red."

"Red what?" I asked, confused.

"You should wear red. It would look really good on you." And she ducked inside the door, not giving me a chance to respond.

When I got home, Daniel was out mowing the lawn. I dropped my books off in my room, and then went out to start the edging. He grinned at me over the mower and waved. We finished about the same time.

As we put the mower and edger away, he wiped the sweat off his forehead. "Thanks for the help, man."

"No problem. Where are Mom and Dad?"

"They went out to get stuff for dinner."

We went in through the garage. I stripped off my shirt.

"I could really go for something cold," Daniel said, heading to the kitchen.

"Me too," I said. I went out onto the back porch, where the shade from the big oak kept it nice and cool.

"Here." He pressed a can into my hand.

I lifted it halfway to my mouth before I realized what it was. "You gave me yours," I said, turning to give him the beer.

He had another one in his hand. He sat down, lifted the can, and grinned at me. "Cheers."

"Dan, I don't want this," I said.

"Mom and Dad aren't around."

"I don't drink," I said, setting the can down on the table in front of him. I went and got myself a soda.

"Sorry, Shadow," he said. "I started drinking when I was fifteen. I figured you did too."

"You know that it bugs Mom and Dad that you drink so much, don't you?" I asked.

"Yeah, I know."

"So why don't you stop, or at least slow down?"

He sighed. "I know I'm not the son they wanted, but it's too late to change. I'm not going to pretend to be somebody I'm not."

"It's never too late to change," I said.

"Wait till you've got a few more years behind you," Dan said. "When you decide to quit wearing black, we can talk about when it's too late to change."

It spooked me that he could see into my head like that.

We were quiet for a few seconds. I was trying to gather the courage to ask him about his Robin.

"So what do you want to do tomorrow?" Dan asked, before I could get my question out.

"What do you mean?"

"I have this feeling Mom will want to do something as a family. Maybe it'd be a good idea to come up with something we'd like to do ahead of time."

"Yeah," I said. "I guess."

We kicked around a few ideas, and finally decided on going to a movie.

"What did you do today?" he asked.

I told him about going to the library and playground with Robin.

"So what's this chick like?"

"She's kind of cute, but really quiet most of the time."

"How long have you known her?"

"Just met her a couple weeks ago. She joined the debate team."

"You going to ask her out again?"

"Probably. Don't say anything about it to Mom and Dad though. They'd want to meet her, and I don't think she's ready for that yet. I know I'm not."

He nodded and kind of grinned.

I hesitated, and then asked, "How long did you date your Robin?"

"Couple of years."

"Wow. That's pretty serious."

"You could say that."

"What was she like?"

He shrugged. "Smart. Cute—you've seen the pictures. She had a great body and a great laugh. She'd always laugh at the stupidest things." He smiled, shaking his head over a private memory. "And she was tough. Because she had to be."

"Why?"

"You don't make it on the streets if you're not tough," he said flatly.

"Oh," I said. "How old was she?"

"A year younger than me."

"Where did she...who...were you living together?"

"Yeah."

"What happened...I mean, how did she die?"

He looked at me for a minute, and I was afraid he was going to walk away again. Instead, he said, "She was stabbed."

"Oh man, that's terrible," I said, wishing I hadn't asked. "I'm so sorry," I added lamely.

He shrugged again, toying with the beer can in his hands. "You really loved her, huh?" I asked.

He took a deep breath, staring at the can. "We were going to have a family together. And it was my fault she died. I should have never..."

"Hey, guys! How about a hand in here!" Mom called from the kitchen.

My mouth was so dry, I couldn't even swallow, let alone say anything to Daniel.

There was a thump as Dad set a few bags on the countertop. "The lawn looks great, Dan," he said.

Dan stood up and headed into the kitchen. "Thanks, Dad," he said. "Shadow helped out."

I didn't get many chances to talk with Daniel for the next two weeks. He had several meetings with the lawyers, and when he was home he always seemed to be sleeping or just zoned out. I stayed late nearly every day after school, practicing different kinds of speeches. I felt more comfortable with the interpretive events than I did with debating. That was Vernon's thing. He teamed up with Lia, Russ, and Ryan to do a Cross-Examination debate late in the week, so Erica, Robin, and I spent our time practicing our events in a separate room.

Erica was pretty good at the interpretive humor readings, and even better at the poetry. But she had a hard time keeping her voice strong, and sometimes when she got flustered, she'd just give up. I could sympathize because it's hard to recover when you let your concentration slip during a speech.

I thought I was about the same level as Erica. I was able to stay calm when presenting, mostly because of Robin's trick of letting my eyes unfocus, but that didn't make it easy. I still hadn't given a speech that met the minimum time standard. My storytelling, although still a little rushed, had gotten better. My impromptu speeches seemed to be missing some "oomph," as Mr. Souza put it. My points were clear enough but I wasn't able to get much passion into my voice.

Neither of us had Robin's gift. She could do a Solo Acting reading, and without a single prop she could make you see the whole town as she walked through it. It was the Creative Storytelling, though, where her talent really shone. Within minutes, she could create a person, conjure up a crisis, and then resolve the problem in the most imaginative way possible.

Mr. Souza watched us more than he let on, and during those last few days before our first meet, he observed at least one speech and one debate by each team member. Our first meet was coming up on Friday, so that meant Wednesday's practice was mandatory if we wanted to go to the meet.

On the way to practice that day, Vernon and I stopped at the school store for a soda. When we reached room 28, Pat was outside the doorway, hanging out with three or four other guys I'd never seen before. He stepped in front of the door as I tried to go through.

"Hey, Shadowman," Pat said. "Your last name's Thompson, right?"

"Yeah," I said, glaring at him.

"You got a brother named Daniel?"

"Yeah," I said. I forced myself to keep eye contact.

"The one who was arrested for murder?"

I broke out in a cold sweat. I wondered if I had missed another article about Daniel in the newspaper.

"What?" one of Pat's buddies exclaimed.

"What are you talking about?" another one asked.

Vernon was looking at me anxiously.

Chapter Nine

"It seems this kid's brother is a killer—"

"He is not." I wanted to shout it, but the words barely even came out. After all, I wasn't sure. Maybe he *was* a killer. He must have done *something* to get arrested.

"Come on, Shadow," Vernon said. "Let's go in."

Pat smirked. He knew he had gotten to me.

Just then Mr. Souza stuck his head out the door. "Will you be joining us, gentlemen? I'd like to finish this practice as soon as possible."

Vernon and I quickly found seats. Pat and his buddies sat a few feet away, whispering to each other. I was sure I knew the topic of their conversation.

It was the biggest practice we'd had all year, because it was mandatory for everyone going to the meet. Almost twenty people were there.

Tess went first. As always, her original oratory dazzled everyone in the room. Everyone except me, that is. I couldn't keep my mind on the speeches. *How did Pat know about Daniel?* I wondered. *Who else already knew?* I tried to concentrate when Lia and Russ performed a Duet Acting, but my mind was racing. *What would people think about my brother?* I managed to listen a little more closely while Robin told an original story—something about fairies living under a mushroom.

Next, Pat was called to the front of the room. That got my attention. He and Vernon did a mock Lincoln-Douglas debate over teen curfews. When the class and Mr. Souza voted Vernon the winner, Pat stormed out of the room.

By the time I drew my choices for an impromptu speech, my mind was churning. I quickly read the sentence: The American Dream has been killed with frivolous lawsuits.

At first I thought it said ferocious, and my heart seemed to stop. Then I read the sentence again. *Frivolous* lawsuits.

I flubbed my way through my speech. Not only was it almost

a minute short, it was so unfocused that it was almost pointless. I just couldn't concentrate.

At the end of practice, I was disappointed, but not surprised, to discover I was not among those who would be competing in our first meet. I congratulated Vernon, Robin, and Lia, the only sophomores who would be going with the team. Mr. Souza reminded us all that there would be many more meets to go to. Before he dismissed us, he emphasized that if any participants could not attend the meet, it was up to them to find a replacement for their event. If they couldn't get someone to go in their place, they'd have to reimburse the school for the entry fee.

"I'm sorry you're not going," Robin said as I walked her home.

I shrugged. "No big deal. I'm not sure I really want to compete in front of a judge anyway," I said. I kicked a stone and it ricocheted off a fence post. "I can't believe Mr. Souza is still taking Pat after he stormed out like that."

"He *is* one of our captains. And he's really good, usually."

I didn't like to hear her stick up for him. "Yeah, but that doesn't give him the right to act like a spoiled brat. Why does he always thinks his speeches are automatically the best?"

"It probably runs in the family. Remember when I said forensics would be good for my career? Pat's here for the same reason. My mother knows Mrs. Riley. Pat's brother's at Harvard Law School, his sister's a big shot D.A. in Denver, and his father's a judge. I'm pretty sure they expect Pat to be a lawyer one day."

"Instead of being a lawyer, he's going to *need* one if he doesn't get a grip on his temper," I said.

We walked in silence for a few moments. I didn't really want to talk about forensics. At least now I knew how Pat knew so much about Daniel. I wondered if Pat's sister was actually involved with the trial.

"How's your brother doing?" Robin asked.

Chapter Nine

"He's all right, I guess," I said, startled by the question. How did she know what I was thinking?

"Why?"

"Just wondering how everything is going. Is his trial soon?"

"Trial starts Friday."

"So you couldn't go to the meet anyway," she said.

"Probably not."

"Probably not?"

"The trial is going to last several days," I said.

"Yeah, but shouldn't you be there for the first day?"

"I'm sure my mom will think so."

"You don't?"

"I don't know. I mean, it's not like he's been around to support *me*. Other than slip me cash from God-knows-where and offer me a beer that I didn't want, he hasn't done jack."

"But he's still your brother. And what about your parents?"

"I'm sick of hearing about my brother. And I don't care what my parents think."

"I thought you said he's been better at home."

"Yeah, he has been. But it's a little too little a little too late, you know?"

She looked at me like she was disappointed or something. But then she said, "I haven't seen anything about it in the papers."

"You've been looking?"

She seemed a little uncomfortable. "I was just curious."

"It's not really a big case, especially here. The Denver paper's keeping up, sort of," I said. "The guy who died was a drug dealer or some other kind of lowlife scum."

"According to your brother?"

"No. He still hasn't told us anything about it. I'm guessing from a comment in a newspaper article I read a few days ago. But as you pointed out, there hasn't been a lot of media coverage up till now." I was grateful for that. There was bound to be more coverage once the trial started. I wondered how it would affect my parents. I wondered how it would affect me.

"Do you still think he did it?"

"I never said I thought that."

She just looked at me.

"I don't know," I said, sticking with the safest phrase. "I don't know any of the details of the case, and I still don't know Daniel."

"You know him better than you did."

"Yeah."

"So has your opinion of him changed?"

"I never had an opinion!" I exclaimed. "I don't know him! I thought I knew him when he was fifteen, but I was wrong. I certainly don't know him now."

"I'm sorry," she said quickly. "It's none of my business."

"It's all right," I said, shrugging it off and watching the ground as we walked on.

"So," she said hesitantly, "what are you doing Saturday night?"

"I don't know."

"Want to do something?"

"Sure," I said, my mind still on Daniel.

"Shadow?" She stopped walking.

I looked back at her and was surprised to see her blushing. I stopped too.

"Are we just friends?"

"What do you mean?"

"I mean, are we just friends, or are we…" She blushed even more.

"Dating?"

She nodded, not looking at me.

I felt my face get hot and wondered if our blushes were matching shades. "What do you want?"

"I asked you first!"

"No, you asked me what we *are*. I'm asking you what you *want* us to be."

She threw her hands up in the air. "Never mind!" She started walking.

I tried not to laugh as I grabbed her hand and stopped her. "I think we've just been friends," I said, "but maybe Saturday night could be a date."

She smiled at me. I heaved a sigh of relief for picking the right answer. We began walking again, still holding hands.

"So what do you want to do?" she asked.

"What?"

"On Saturday. What do you want to do?"

"Oh. I don't know," I said. "Go see a movie maybe?"

"Sounds good."

That evening, Daniel was in a terrible mood. He snapped at Mom three times during dinner and once at Dad. He virtually ignored me. Instead of helping clean up after dinner, he just sat in the living room and steadily drank his way through two six-packs.

The tension level had been increasing in our house all week, and by eight o'clock it was almost as high it had been when Daniel first came home.

I was grateful to have a load of homework to do. As I was excusing myself to go work, Dad stopped me.

"How's forensics going?"

"Pretty good," I said. I didn't really think he was interested in forensics. I figured he was trying to make up for the awkward lack of conversation at dinner.

"Is it getting easier to speak in front of people?"

"A little bit," I said. "But so far I'm just speaking in front of Mr. Souza and the other team members. I don't know what it will be like in front of strangers and judges."

"When's the first meet?" Mom asked. "Do they need any parent volunteers?"

"They're always looking for volunteers. Our first meet is on Friday—"

"You can't go on Friday!" Mom interrupted. "Absolutely not!"

"But I'm not—"

"No, Shadow. You can't go. This is not open for discussion."

I was furious she cut me off like that. Never mind the fact that I wasn't on the team chosen to go. She hadn't even given me a chance to explain. My anger boiled up to the surface. "I've spent the last month getting ready!" I shouted. "It means a lot more to me than the first day of some stupid trial!"

"Shadow!" Mom gasped.

I felt rotten for saying that in front of Daniel, but it was true. "He won't even talk to us about what happened! Why should he care if we're there or not? Why should I want to be there?"

Mom and Dad just stared at me for a minute.

"Let him go," Daniel said from his corner. "He's got his own life."

"He's got a family," Mom said firmly. "And family is the most important thing."

"I haven't been a part of this family for a long time," Daniel said. "And I'll be out of it again soon."

"Why?" Mom asked, turning toward him with tears in her eyes. "Why do you keep saying that? Why have you given up?"

Daniel looked at her. "Because I know what I'm charged with, and I know what I did. And I'd do it again if I got the chance."

Mom got very pale. Dad was watching Daniel with a blank look on his face.

You really did it. I wanted to say the words, but nothing would come out. This was what I had been afraid of all along.

He was my brother. He was sitting less than fifteen feet away from me. And he had killed a man.

Chapter Ten

At school the next day, I couldn't focus on anything. I vaguely remembered going into my room and doing my trig homework after Daniel's bombshell the night before, but when it came time to turn in our assignment, I couldn't find anything in my folder. In chemistry and American lit the teachers called on me, confident I would have the answer as always. I didn't even understand the questions they were asking. The day was over before I could formulate a coherent thought.

The Denver paper had run a longer article about the upcoming trial that morning. This one mentioned that Reggie DiGallo was a known gang member, and that the altercation with Daniel may have been either gang or drug related. DiGallo had been stabbed twice, once in the leg and once in the chest. The last paragraph said that our family had no comment.

I was in a daze. All I could hear, over and over again, was Daniel's voice. *I know what I'm charged with, and I know what I did. And I'd do it again if I got the chance.* His words had sounded so cold, so uncaring. The tone he had used the first couple of days was back, and so was the distance. He hadn't come to my room to talk for four nights in a row. It was as if any progress we had made had been erased.

I know what I'm charged with, and I know what I did. And I'd do it again if I got the chance.

As I looked back, I realized that I had started to open up to Daniel, and I thought he had been opening up to me. He had told me about his Robin; he had even teased me a little about my Robin. I had to admit that I had started to care about him again.

But how could I care about someone who had torn our family apart?

How could I care about a killer?

I know what I'm charged with, and I know what I did. And I'd do it again if I got the chance.

What would make a person want to kill someone? What kind of person kills without regret? I couldn't imagine stabbing someone, being face to face with them as they died. The overwhelming feeling that I didn't know Daniel at all washed over me again.

After school I decided to skip forensics practice. It would be too depressing, watching everyone else practice for tomorrow's meet. And besides, I still couldn't focus on anything. Walking along the street, I let my mind drift again. Daniel had admitted to selling drugs, hustling pool, and gambling. None of those were activities I could respect. But, I had to admire him a little. I could only imagine how tough living on the street must have been. He had never asked for help from anyone; he had survived on his own.

And as we had talked about our Robins, I had begun to look at him in a different way. It was clear that he had really loved her, and that they had both been trying to change their lives for the better.

I nearly jumped out of my skin when a hand came down on my shoulder from behind.

"God, Shadow, why are you so jumpy? Didn't you hear me calling?"

I shook my head. "What are you doing here?"

"Looking for you," Daniel said, falling into step with me.

"Why?"

"I wanted to make sure that you're going to go to your meet tomorrow."

"Why?" I asked again.

"'Cause of what you said last night. You've worked hard for this. It means a lot to you." He shrugged. "It's more important for you to be at the meet than it is for you to be at the trial," he said.

"You mean you don't want me there."

He stopped and gave me a sad little grin. "You cut right through the crap and call it straight, don't you? Okay," he said, looking me in the eye. "You're right. I don't want you there. I don't want Mom and Dad there either."

"Why not?" I didn't understand why he wouldn't want us there, why he wouldn't want the moral support.

"Because of the things that will be said. You guys don't need to hear any of it."

"Maybe we do," I replied evenly. "And it looks like we're never going to hear anything from you. The only way we'll ever hear it is at the trial."

"Look, Shadow, it's not a lot of cool stuff."

"I know," I said. "But it's part of where you've been, part of what's taken you away from us for the last seven years. It might make things easier if you'd just talk to us."

"I never should have called," he muttered.

"Then why did you?" I asked bluntly. We were standing in the middle of the sidewalk, in the middle of the block. This was hardly the time or place to have this discussion, but I wasn't going to let him get away again without telling me something.

He spread his hands helplessly. "I...I wanted to say I'm sorry. I didn't want Mom and Dad to find out through the papers. I owed them at least that much. I wanted to...maybe...I just wanted to say I'm sorry."

"You can't just call up to say you're sorry and expect to be forgiven right away, especially when it's something this big."

"I didn't know what else to do. And anyway, I'm not looking for forgiveness."

"Then why apologize?"

He shrugged again. "I don't know," he said in a tone eerily like mine.

"Well, I'll be there tomorrow anyway," I said. "I'm not going to the meet."

"I wish you would. It's not just that I don't want you at the trial," he added quickly. "It's time for you and Mom and Dad to look to the future, not the past. That's all this trial is. Crap from the past."

"But the past is all part of who we are. If we understand our past, maybe we can have a better future."

He looked at me long and hard. "That's a nice thought, Shadow, but it doesn't look as if I have much of a future now." He turned away from me. "They'll never believe me." He spoke so quietly the noise of the passing traffic almost swept his words away. "Besides, I did it. I killed him."

I wanted to shut my ears. I wanted to run away and never come back.

"My only regret is I didn't do it sooner. I was too late."

I hesitated, almost afraid to ask. "Too late for what?"

He looked around at me. I had never seen him look so desperate. "To save Robin. To save our family."

"You mean the guy you killed?..."

"I came home from the pool hall one afternoon. I was way behind on payments to DiGallo, and he was pounding on my apartment door. I had told him I didn't want him around my girl, and I shouted at him to get away from our apartment. He started yelling back about the cash I owed him. Robin opened the door, telling us to shut up before someone called the cops. Reggie pushed his way inside.

"He started waving this big knife around, saying that he'd get the money out of me one way or another. I told Robin to go into our bedroom, but she wouldn't listen to me. By that time Reggie was in a full-blown fit. He was a wild man. I was trying to calm him down, to edge him toward the door, when he started lunging at me with the knife. Robin ran over, screaming at us to stop—she never could stand fights—and the next thing I knew, she was on the floor, bleeding." Daniel stared at the sidewalk. "I'm not sure about what happened next. I think I tackled Reggie. I must have knocked the knife out of his hand, because I remember picking it up. All I could think of was that he had hurt Robin. I guess I stabbed him. When he fell, I went over to help Robin."

I had to strain to hear his next words.

"I was too late. She never regained consciousness." He took a deep breath and let the air out in a long sigh. "We were gonna move, get out of town and start over, go someplace safe. But we were too late. I lost my family."

"Your family?" I asked, bewildered. "You mean..."

"What do you think I mean?"

I turned in a slow circle. I wanted to sit down, to absorb everything. Daniel was going to be a father? I would have been an uncle?

"Oh, Dan," I finally said. "I'm so sorry."

"Me too," he said with a weak grin and hard eyes. "Me too. And the worst part is, it was all my fault. If it hadn't been for me, Robin would still be alive."

"But you tried to help her—"

"No. I mean I was the one who got us into trouble in the first place."

"I think you should tell Mom and Dad," I said.

"No," he said. "I couldn't stand it if they—" He broke off and started again. "It doesn't matter what happens to me now. I wish I'd never called them."

Hearing him say that was like a blow to the gut. I thought we were doing better. I thought we were all finally trying. And now he was going to quit. "Daniel, Mom and—"

"Just do me a favor and keep bein' a good kid. They don't need any more grief."

He turned away and started down the sidewalk.

"Daniel," I called to him. "Wait."

He just kept walking.

The house was empty and quiet. I dropped my books on my desk and then went straight to Daniel's room. The door was slightly ajar. The CD case was still on the dresser, but the only photo in it was of Daniel and Robin. I studied their faces carefully. They sure looked happy together. I looked around the room. Daniel had lost Robin and their future family, so he called his past family. But I guess we weren't enough to ease the ache he had inside.

I had resented Daniel for coming back and upsetting our lives. I had been angry at him for using Mom and Dad's money, especially when he kept them at such a distance and gave so little in return. But now I could see that when Daniel had called, he'd never expected anyone to believe in him enough to care.

He never expected our help.

He never believed we still loved him.

Suddenly I couldn't handle being alone in the house. I wrote a quick note for Mom and Dad, telling them I was at the library and would be home in time for dinner.

"Shadow!"

In spite of myself, I jumped again. "Dan? Man, you've got to—" I broke off. It was Dad. He had pulled up in his car and was waiting across the street. I checked my watch. I wasn't late.

I jogged over. "Hey," I said, climbing in the passenger side.

Chapter Ten

"What are you doing here?"

"I saw your note. Thought you might want a ride home. Looks like it might rain."

"Thanks," I said, looking doubtfully at the clear sky.

"Music?" Dad asked, turning on the radio. He flipped through the preset stations, which were all talk radio, and then hit scan until some tunes came on. He turned up the volume.

The look on his face stopped me from asking what was wrong, even when we passed the entrance to our development. I knew this had to have something to do with Daniel. A few minutes later, we were pulling into the parking lot of JR Rockers'.

The lot was nearly empty, so we were able to pull into a spot right in front of the building. Dad turned the engine off, but then he just sat there. I didn't know what to say.

"I uh—" Dad cleared his throat. "Dan wasn't home yet, and I knew your mother would panic if he was late again tonight, so— I'm just going to run in and see if he's here."

"Okay," I said, and for some reason my voice sounded small.

Dad stared at the entrance to the bar. After a few seconds, he kind of shook himself all over and got out of the car.

I turned around and studied the marquee of the cheap movie theater across the street. Maybe I could take Robin to see a movie next week.

Dad wasn't inside very long. By the time I looked back toward the bar, the door was open and Dad was backing out of it, pulling Daniel with him. My brother didn't seem to be arguing with Dad so much as still trying to talk to someone in the bar.

As the door swung shut behind them, Daniel turned around and started walking, so Dad let go of his arm. Almost immediately, Dan stumbled and fell.

I started to unbuckle my seatbelt, but then Dad waved me off and shook his head. He was bending over to help Daniel up when the door to the bar flew open.

Two big guys, looking like they had just stepped out of an old Hell's Angels flick, started yelling at Daniel. They looked almost identical, both wearing black leather and bushy mustaches. The only difference I could see at a glance was one wore a red bandana and the other heavier man wore an orange one. Dad was so startled, he let Daniel fall back down. The guy in the red bandana actually lifted Daniel up off the ground.

I was having a hard time locating the seat belt buckle release, so I had to look down and see what I was doing. When I looked up again, Daniel was back on the ground, writhing now, and Dad was trying to get between him and the two men.

The door handle seemed to have moved, because I had to look down to find it, too. Finally I got the car door open.

"—asshole owes me—" one of the guys was saying.

"Do not!" Daniel moaned from the ground.

The bigger man with the orange bandana tried to lunge past Dad, who somehow managed to stop him. Considering he had at least a hundred pounds on Dad, I was impressed.

"Wait, wait, can we please talk about it?" Dad said.

The other guy put a hand on the stocky one's arm, and I think he would have stopped him, except Daniel suddenly came flying at both of them.

He had the advantage of surprise, and he knocked the orange bandana guy flat on his back. The other one gave my father a shocked look before he pulled his arm back and decked him.

"Dad!" I yelled and ran toward them. The man standing over my dad stopped and stared at me.

"What the hell do you think you're doing, bringin' your kid to a bar?" he asked my dad.

"Trying to bring my other kid home," Dad grunted, holding a hand over his cheek.

The man looked over his shoulder to where his buddy and Dan were rolling on the ground, trying to beat the crap out of each other. "He hustled us," he said by way of explanation to my dad. "If we ever see him here again…"

I helped Dad up, but then just clung to his arm. I couldn't move.

"I'll be sure to explain it to him," Dad said. "Could you just call off your friend before he kills him?"

"Yo, Percy! Let's go!"

Orange bandana gave Daniel one more blow to the head, and then stood up. He pulled his leather vest down, hawked a loogie that just missed landing on Daniel, and walked into the bar without a backward glance. Red bandana followed.

"You okay, Shadow?" Dad asked.

"Huh?" I was looking to make sure the two guys weren't coming back. "Oh. Yeah, I'm okay. I didn't get hit."

"Then maybe you could let go of me," he said, gently prying my hand off his arm.

My brother groaned and rolled on to his side. We helped him up and somehow got him into the car. I climbed into the back seat, numb.

The ride home was absolutely silent. I wasn't sure if Daniel was still conscious, the way his head lolled around. He was trashed in more ways than one. I could smell the alcohol, even under the cigarette smoke. Through the rearview mirror, I could see that he was a mess. There were several cuts and bruises on his face, and his shirt was filthy. My heart sank. He really was beyond our help.

In the garage, it was impossible to tell if Daniel was staggering because he was hurt or because he was drunk. Dad and I followed him into the house. Mom called hello from the living room. My brother made it as far as the front entryway, where he sat down, hard.

"Ow," he said, looking up at us with bleary eyes.

"Oh, Daniel," Mom moaned. She hurried off to the kitchen,

and came back quickly with a damp cloth. She tried to clean his face, but he kept jerking away.

"Stop it, Mom," he complained.

"But, Daniel," she whispered, reaching for his face again. He slapped her hand away.

"Caroline," Dad said, lifting her up off her knees.

"Call me Dan." My brother's voice was slurred, but it had an angry edge. "I'm not your little boy anymore."

"No, you're not," Dad said. "Why don't you go get yourself cleaned up?"

He struggled for a minute, trying to get up off the floor. Mom tried to step forward, but Dad held her back. Daniel finally got to his feet. He took a few wobbly steps, then turned to look at me. "You going to your...your speech thing?"

I just stared at him. He was too disgusting for words.

"Shadow will be at the trial," Mom said to his back. "We'll *all* be there."

"I don't want you there!" Daniel exploded. "It's my life, my problem. Just let me deal with it!"

"You need us—" Mom began in a trembling voice.

"No," Daniel cut in harshly. "I don't need you. I haven't needed you since I was fifteen. That hasn't changed." He turned a little too sharply, pushed himself off the wall, and then continued to stagger down the hall.

The phone rang at the same time his door slammed shut. Dad grabbed it before the answering machine could pick up. "Hello? Yes.... Who?"

"Shadow," he said curtly, returning his attention to Mom.

I took the phone, still trying to digest what had just happened. "Hello?"

"Shadow?" The voice was a hoarse whisper.

"Yeah?"

"It's Tess."

Chapter Ten

"Hi," I said in surprise. I wrenched my attention from my parents' whispered conversation and tried to focus on Tess's raspy voice.

"Look, I hate to do this to you, but you're my last chance." She tried to clear her throat. "I've lost my voice and I can't go to the meet tomorrow. Could you take my place?"

"I don't know. I haven't practiced much."

"Please. I've called everyone, and no one else can go."

"What are your events?"

"I'm doing Impromptu and a Cross-Examination debate with Pat."

"Um…"

"Please, Shadow!" she said hoarsely. "Please?"

I looked around. Mom and Dad were still whispering together. Daniel had told me to go to the meet. He had said he didn't want me at the trial. There was nothing I could do to stop his self-destruction. I spoke before I could change my mind again. "Sure," I blurted out. "I'll take your spot."

"Thank you! You know when the bus leaves and everything?"

"Yeah."

"Okay. Well, good luck. And would you tell Mr. Souza I'm sorry? I'll talk to him about it on Monday," she rasped.

"Okay. Hope you feel better."

"Thanks. Good-bye."

"Bye."

I hung up the phone.

Mom was staring down the hallway. Dad was watching her with a concerned expression.

"Um…hey," I said, uncertain how to begin.

Dad glanced at me.

"One of the girls on the forensics team got sick. She needed someone to take her spot at the meet tomorrow."

Mom tore her eyes away from the empty hallway. "Surely you didn't say you'd go!"

"Yeah," I said defensively, "I did."

"Well, call that girl back right now," she snapped. "You can't go tomorrow."

"I *have* to go now!" I exclaimed.

At the same instant Dad said, "Caroline, I think that—"

"We're all going to be there for Daniel," she said, ignoring us both.

"He doesn't want us there!" I was almost shouting. "Weren't you listening?"

"He didn't mean it." Her voice was now calm, almost serene.

"Yes, he did!"

"Caroline," Dad tried again, but Mom wouldn't let him finish.

"No," she insisted. "He's been drinking. He doesn't know what he's saying."

"He said the same thing this afternoon when I saw him after school. He was sober then!" I retorted.

"Shadow, I'm not going to argue with you!"

"Good! I'm not going to argue with you, either! I'm going to the meet!"

"How can you abandon your brother that way?" Mom yelled.

"What about him? He abandoned us for seven years!"

"Shadow," Dad began, his tone a warning.

"How can you support him?" I demanded. "How can he be so important? How can you love him so much, after all he's done to us? Look at him! He's nothing but a strung-out, drunken—"

"That's enough!" Dad finally shouted. Mom and I both looked at him. "Maclean called me the other day and suggested family counseling. I'm beginning to think he was right. We can't handle this by ourselves. But we need to be able to sit down and talk *now,*" he said, trying to use his normal tone.

Mom started toward the couch, but I shook my head. "I'm out of here," I said.

Chapter Ten

"What?" Dad asked sharply.

"Maybe if I leave, what *I* want will become important too." I darted through the front door and slammed it behind me.

I took off running. I cut through a couple of yards, in case they tried to follow me. It only took me a few minutes to get to Vernon's house. I rang the doorbell and his younger sister answered.

"Is Vernon here?"

"Yeah," she said, sounding uncertain.

"Could I talk to him for a minute?"

She gave me a strange look before she disappeared into the house.

"Hey, man," Vernon said, appearing from around a corner. "What's up?"

"Could I come in?"

"Sure."

"Thanks."

I followed him back to his room.

"What's up?" he asked again. "You forget your trig book or something?"

"Any chance I can crash here tonight?" I blurted out.

"Here?" He looked surprised. "Um...I guess. What's going on? You look...really wild."

I could imagine how my face must look right now. "Big fight with my parents," I said, sitting down on his bed. "I just need a place to stay for the night."

"I've got to leave early tomorrow," he said hesitantly. "You know, for the meet." I could tell he felt bad about going to the meet when I wasn't.

I nodded. "I'm going too. Tess can't make it, and she asked me to take her spot."

A big grin lit up Vernon's face. "Really? Cool!"

"Yeah. Of course, I was her last choice, but—"

"Who cares? At least you're going now!"

"So will it be a problem if I stay?"

"Nah," he said, shaking his head. "This is perfect. I'll just tell my parents that it'll make it easier since we both have to leave so early. Let me go tell them you're here. Want anything to eat?"

I shrugged. I hadn't eaten dinner yet, but I didn't want to be a mooch. I wasn't sure my stomach could handle any food right now anyway.

"I was just going to grab a snack," he said. "I'll be right back." He left me alone in his room for about fifteen minutes. When he came back, he had six sandwiches, a bag of chips, a stack of cookies, and two Cokes. My mouth started watering as soon as I saw the tray. "This should keep us for a while," he said.

"This is a snack? If you eat like this, I'm surprised you're not a lot bigger than I am," I said. "Or at least a lot wider." I picked up a sandwich.

"So," Vernon said, "what happened?"

Briefly I explained the argument that had followed the fight at the bar. I thought about calling home, but I changed my mind.

"He got drunk again? I thought he was cleaning up his act."

"That's what I thought too," I said. "And I believe he was for a while. But I guess he just doesn't care."

"It sounds like he's trying to push you away."

"Sounds like it? He came right out and said he was."

"Yeah, but I mean, it sounds like he thinks it will be better for you and your parents not to be close to him. You know, like that guy on *ER*—or was it on *The Practice*? Well, anyway, this guy found out he was dying, and he tried to push everyone away, so when he died it wouldn't hurt the others as much."

"Maybe. But I don't think that's it. I think he just doesn't want us in his way."

Chapter Ten

We finished our sandwiches quickly and quietly. Then we did some prep work for the meet.

Vernon had copied a bunch of stuff from the files, and had it spread out on his desk. He offered to share and also told me I could use his computer to surf the net for more info if I wanted to. I hadn't done much with the debates other than watch and judge them. I hoped I could get by with one night of cramming. As we finished the chips, a new dilemma occurred to me. I hadn't had a chance to get clean clothes or anything. "Hey, I don't suppose you have an extra shirt that might fit me? For tomorrow?"

Vernon made a face at me. "Sure, you think the shrimp is going to have some shirts big enough for the bean pole?" He shook his head. Then he said, "My brother's almost as tall as you. Let me go see if I can snag one from him."

He came back a few minutes later, carrying three shirts. "You can try these. I couldn't find anything black."

There was a white button-down, a green sweatshirt, and a red polo. I pulled on the polo shirt. It fit just fine.

The next morning, we left early for the meet. So early, in fact, it was still dark out. Neither of us wanted to take the time to eat, so we just grabbed a couple of bagels and headed out. We walked toward the school in silence. After a few minutes, Vernon spoke up. "You okay, Shadow? You don't look so good. "

"I didn't sleep very well."

"I said you could take the bed—"

"It wasn't because I was on the floor. The sleeping bag was fine. I was just too worked up last night to sleep. I kept expecting my parents to call or barge in your front door."

He stared at the ground. "Well, actually, when I went to get the sandwiches, I called them."

"You what?"

"I just thought, given what your family has already been through, it would be better if they at least knew where you were."

"Thanks," I muttered. Half of me was upset by what he had done, but the other half appreciated it.

When we got to the school, Mr. Souza was standing in front of the bus, signing people in. I explained to him that I would be taking Tess's events for the day. I could sense his disappointment even though he tried to hide it.

"I'll do the best I can," I said.

"I'm sure you will, Shadow."

Vernon and I climbed onto the bus. I expected exaggerated gasps when people saw the red shirt, but no one said anything. We took the seat in front of Robin and Lia.

"What are you doing here?" asked Lia.

I went through the explanation again about Tess asking me to take her place.

Robin looked at me carefully. "I thought you had something else to do today."

"Nope," I said, not meeting her eyes.

Vernon asked Robin and Lia a question about one of the events, and soon the three of them were talking excitedly about the meet. I leaned my head against the window and watched the sun come up.

I knew I should try to prepare for Tess's—*my* events, but I couldn't stop thinking about Daniel. Had he gotten drunk last night just so he'd be able to sleep it off instead of spending the entire night thinking about the trial? No matter the outcome of the trial, Daniel had a hard road ahead of him, and he would have to travel it alone. Either he would be found guilty and would have to spend years in jail, or he would be found not guilty, and he would have to come to terms with his alcoholism, loss, and screwed-up life. This could be one of his last days with any kind of freedom. *The next time I see him,* I thought, *we might be looking through a thick plastic window, talking to each other on a phone.*

Maybe Vernon was right. Maybe Daniel really was trying to make it easier for us by pushing us away. He had been gone for so long and had become so used to relying on himself that he didn't realize how much it hurt Mom and Dad when he wouldn't let them get close to him.

"Shadow?"

I looked back over the bus seat.

Robin was leaning forward. "Are you all right?" she asked in a low voice.

I nodded.

"You sure? You look kind of upset."

I tried to grin for her. "I'll be all right. I just don't feel like talking right now."

She flashed a small smile at me. "Okay. I'm here if you need me."

"Thanks."

When we got to the meet, we followed the upperclassmen to the registration tables. We were given times and room assignments for each event. Robin, Lia, Vernon, and I got back together to compare assignments. I was the only one with an eight o'clock event, so they decided they'd come be my moral support. Vernon and Lia had ten o'clock events. Robin's event was after the lunch break. If my debate finished in time, I just might get to see her do the storytelling.

Together we headed toward the room for Impromptu Speaking. It was my favorite event during practice, but I was really nervous. I wished I could watch some other events before I had to speak.

We found the presentation room. A woman with a clipboard

was directing the participants into a separate side room where we were to pick up our cards and prepare our speeches.

As Vernon and Lia went through the door to the presentation room, Robin kind of hung back. "Remember," she told me, "look toward the audience, but don't look at them."

"I'll let my eyes unfocus," I said.

She shifted from one foot to the other. "I was right, you know," she said shyly.

"About what?"

"About red. You look really good today." Robin blushed almost the same shade as the polo. She took a step toward me, reached up, and kissed me quickly on the cheek. "Good luck," she said.

Chapter Eleven

In the side room, there was a hushed air of tension. It felt like we were all waiting for a final exam, but none of us had been allowed to study. The woman went over the rules and gave us each different times to go and draw our topics. I had twenty minutes to wait. The event was carefully structured so each speaker had no more than five minutes to prepare. We could write notes on a 3x5 card, but we couldn't bring anything else with us for the presentation.

I set my cards aside, afraid that if I allowed myself to touch them, they'd be shredded before my name was called. With increasing nerves, I watched the other students draw their topics. They would write feverishly, then disappear into the room next door, where the judge and audience were waiting. I was beginning to regret eating the bagel.

Finally, it was my turn.

I stared at the piece of paper I had drawn. Three topics were listed—a word, a phrase, and a sentence. I had to choose one. The sentence was "California's 'three-strikes' law is unjust." That one held promise; I had brought in a few articles about it for our files at school, and I thought I could remember some specific information. The phrase was "character education." I discounted that one. As far as I knew, I had never received any structured character education.

The word was "forgiveness."

That stopped me cold. It felt like my brain skidded to a halt. Of all the words for me to draw in a competition, why would I get that one? I looked back at the sentence. I didn't have to do the word. So why was I looking at it again? I only had five minutes to prepare a three- to five-minute speech; I didn't have any time for indecisiveness.

I put my pencil tip on a 3x5 card, but I couldn't write anything. My mind was a murky fog. My thoughts were jumbled; I couldn't make sense out of any of them. I waited for my pencil to start writing anything about three strikes, but it just sat there and my 3x5 card remained blank.

"Shadow Thompson."

I jumped and looked at the judge.

"You're up."

In disbelief I stared at the clock. My five minutes had evaporated, and I had nothing on my card, nothing in my brain.

Numbly, I got up and followed the judge into the room. Mr. Souza was probably somewhere in the back of the room. So were Lia, Robin, and Vernon. I didn't look, just scanned the room. If I let myself see individual faces, I'd never make it.

I handed the topic paper to the judge.

"Which one will you be doing?" she asked.

"I'll use the sentence." I just wished I knew what I'd use it for.

She marked her ballot. I went to the podium at the front of the room. My mouth was dry and I wasn't sure I'd be able to speak at all. The judge must have had the same thought, because she cleared her throat and nodded toward me.

"California's 'three-strikes' law is unjust." I folded the blank card in half and put it in my pocket. "In the first place," I began, forcing myself to look straight ahead, "basing a law on a baseball expression is ridiculous. After a player strikes out, he knows he'll have another chance his next time at bat. When someone is convicted under the three strikes law, he never gets another chance. 'Three strikes' is a bad idea for a law."

I felt pretty good. I wasn't sure where I was going with this, but my voice hadn't broken and my heartbeat had calmed down. I was seeing a very unfocused room in front of me—nothing but shapes and colors.

"This law implies that people can't reform...that they can't learn from their mistakes." I paused for a second to take a deep breath. "Imagine someone who has been imprisoned twice for a crime like petty theft. He serves his time, gets out, and stays clean for years. Then he makes one mistake, and he has to pay with the rest of his life. Even if all three of his offenses have been petty theft, he gets locked up. That's it. No more chances.

"I think people can reform if they are given a fair chance. They shouldn't have to spend the rest of their lives looking over their shoulders. The three strikes law is...well, it's unforgiving."

Do all criminals deserve to be forgiven?

"After three strikes," I went on, "a juvenile offender who has been caught shoplifting the third time could spend the next fifty years in jail." I paused. Now that I'd said it, I wasn't so sure. Maybe juvenile offenders didn't fall under the three strikes law. I felt panic begin to creep in.

"Um...even hardened career criminals deserve a second chance." I plowed on, hoping to regain my train of thought. "Or, rather, they deserve more than a second or third chance. They deserve however many chances it takes to get their lives together." I was sinking. I couldn't believe what I had just heard myself say.

"Doesn't that sound stupid?" I asked, trying to show that I was being sarcastic. "Some people really think that way. But you...but we can't keep giving criminals more chances to harm people. Yeah, the first time it was only shoplifting, but that's a...a gateway crime. The next one could be a mugging, a rape...or even a murder."

We gave Daniel a second chance. He blew it. Why should he get a third?

I had to fight to keep my mind on the speech.

"Well, then, is three strikes too many? Should we lock all criminals up forever?

"No. We can't do that. And we can't let them all go. So what do we do? Maybe three strikes is the best we can do."

I felt like I had been talking for days. But the logical part of my mind knew only seconds had passed.

"In a perfect world, there's no crime, no broken families, no hungry people. In a perfect world, no one gets hurt, and parents and kids love each other no matter what. No one ever has to say they're sorry. No one has to ask for forgiveness.

Daniel left me.

"But this world isn't perfect. People do get hurt and they get hurt by other people."

Daniel hurt me.

"And we look for someone to blame, for someone to pay the price. Sometimes, there's no one who can be blamed, but we try anyway. We won't accept an apology. We want someone's time, someone's tears, someone's blood. Even though the crime may have been committed out of need, out of desperation, out of...some kind of basic human survival instincts, we still demand that someone pay for it."

Why can't I forgive Daniel? Doesn't he deserve another chance?

"Maybe making laws is our way to balance out an imperfect world. Maybe we need to give people a chance to apologize, to make up for what they have done. And maybe sometimes people deserve more than three chances."

Daniel's my brother. The only one I'll ever have.

I rushed through my concluding sentence. "We're all flawed, and therefore so is our justice system. But as flawed as our laws are, we need them, even when they fall short of achieving the for-giveness and redemption that truly matter."

I drew a deep breath. I felt like I had run a hard mile. I couldn't remember much of what I said, and I was pretty convinced that I had rambled off course, that the speech didn't have a tight coherent message. But that didn't matter to me. What mattered was that I had finally realized that I could forgive Daniel. I had to find a way to tell him before it was too late.

Through the light, polite applause, I walked back to where Robin and the others were waiting. Mr. Souza stopped me.

He was smiling. "Nice job, Shadow."

"Really?" I asked.

He shrugged. "Well, you did wander a bit. You should have stated your thesis a little more clearly and stuck with it, but you maintained eye contact, and your voice carried the emotion with-out getting overly dramatic. I'd say it was a decent first competi-tion speech."

"Thank you," I said. "Um, Mr. Souza, I need to go."

"Go? Go where?"

"I have an appointment I need to go to."

"What about your debate?"

"I'll pay for the registration cost," I began.

"I can cover your CX debate," Robin said quickly.

"Thanks," I said, relieved. Hopefully there would be a bus stop nearby. If I could get to the Greyhound station, I might be able to get to Denver by early afternoon.

Mr. Souza was shaking his head. "I'm sorry, Shadow, I can't let you go without parent permission."

I opened my mouth to argue, but a hand came down on my shoulder.

"He has it."

"Dad?" I turned around to stare in disbelief at my father.

165

He grinned at me, then held out his hand to Mr. Souza. "Mark Thompson, Shadow's father. I'm sorry to take him away from here, but we have a family emergency."

"Oh, of course," Mr. Souza said quickly, shaking Dad's hand. "Well, in that case…I hope everything is okay."

"Thank you," Dad said. "I do too." He put his arm around my shoulders and gave me a brief squeeze as we walked toward the doors.

"I'm very proud of you, Shadow. That was an impressive speech. How long had you been working on it?"

"About thirty seconds." I laughed. "It was impromptu. I'm not even sure I remember what I said."

He squeezed me again with his arm. "I sure wish your mother and brother could have heard you."

"Thanks, Dad, for letting me do at least that event."

"I would have let you stay for the rest, if you'd wanted to," he said. "Your mother and I had a long discussion last night after Vernon called. We decided that we need to be supporting you as much as we need to support Daniel."

"You don't think we'll be too late, do you, Dad?" I asked as we left the building.

"No, Shadow. I don't think so."

Chapter Twelve

The judge slammed the gavel down. Everyone around me stood, glad for the ten-minute recess. Maclean's opening statement and various motions had taken the better part of the afternoon.

Mom and Dad leaned over the rail that split the courtroom, talking urgently with Maclean. Daniel was standing a few feet away, pointedly ignoring the guard who took steps that mirrored his.

I stood up and moved over to the rail next to Daniel.

"What are you doing here? Thought you were going to your speech thing."

"I was," I stammered. "I mean, I went, but I...I decided—"

"I wish they had let you go," he interrupted, ignoring my sputtered protests. "Man, I'll be glad when it's all over." He glanced at me. "I'm sure you're just as eager to get this over with."

"What do you mean?"

"As soon as the jury's verdict comes in, you'll finally be able to decide how you feel about me."

"Dan, that's not—"

"I'm sorry," he said quickly, interrupting me. "That wasn't fair. You've been incredibly cool, considering the circumstances," he finished with a twisted grin.

"Thanks," I said. "And I wanted to talk to you about—"

"I never should have called."

"No, Dan, don't—"

"Your life would be so much better if I had just stayed gone."

"Would you let me speak!" I suddenly burst out. The guard and the prosecutor looked over at us, but everyone else was still involved in their own conversations. Forcing myself to lower my voice, I continued, "That's what I wanted to talk to you about."

"What?"

"I'm really glad you called, Dan."

The disbelief was plain on his face. "Shad, you don't have to BS me."

"No, let me finish! I never even realized how angry at you I was when you left, at least not until you came back. We needed you back. I didn't know how much I really missed you until you came home, and now—" I stopped, choking on the tears I promised myself I wouldn't cry any more.

Suddenly he reached across the rail and pulled me into a rough hug. I almost started bawling right there. He clapped me twice, hard, on the back, and then stepped back. His eyes were glistening.

He cleared his throat twice, then said, "Thanks, Shadow, for giving me a chance. I'll do my best not to blow it this time. But whatever the verdict," Dan continued, "I won't be around for a while."

Startled, I asked, "Why not?"

"I need some help. No, I need a lot of help. If Maclean can convince the jury to believe the truth, then I'm going straight to rehab. I need to get cleaned up so I can go to my brother's speech meets and understand what's going on."

"You're going to rehab?"

"Yeah," he said, and his face was pale. "It might kill me, not being able to drink the pain away, but at least I won't cause you and Mom and Dad any more."

"Dan—"

"It's true," he said harshly. "I've been so selfish all my life. It's time for me to do something for someone else. Time for me to do something for the people who care about me."

Chapter Twelve

"Taking care of yourself is all we want you to do."

"Thanks." Maclean was motioning to him, and Daniel stepped toward him before stopping to say, "Oh, hey, could I borrow that tie Mom bought for you a couple of days ago? The one with the race cars?"

"I thought you said it was for a little kid!"

"Yeah, but sometimes bein' a little kid ain't all that bad."

"You'd look great in that tie," Mom whispered, "if you'd just stop fidgeting with it!"

I was wearing my black dress pants and black silk shirt, with a red tie. I thought I looked pretty good too. Dan had said I looked like a pimp.

Mom and Dad were alternating nights in Denver with Daniel; the judge wanted him staying in town. I had made it to Denver as many times as I could during the trial. After the first three days, the quiet in the courtroom had really gotten to me. The lawyers' speeches and questioning techniques were interesting, but in between there were long lulls. If it had been my butt on the line I would have started begging for mercy the first day. Daniel just sat quietly, separated from us by the court banister.

This was the last day of the trial, though, and I was listening carefully to every word. My nerves were shot by the time the prosecuting attorney finished his closing arguments and sat down. Mr. Maclean, Daniel's lawyer, shuffled some papers. He leaned over to whisper to Daniel and patted him on the shoulder. Maclean stood up and wandered over to the jury.

"Ladies and gentlemen, in the last few days you have heard about three lives that have been lost—Reggie DiGallo, Robin Grant, and her unborn child. And there's nothing that can be done about that tragedy. But a fourth life now hangs in the balance, and that you *can* do something about.

"My client has not led an ideal life, and he's made mistakes. He

169

ran away from home at fifteen, and he's been paying for it ever since. Along the way, he learned how to survive. He did his share of drugs, hustling, and gambling. That's how he got involved with Reggie DiGallo, collecting money for him."

I looked over at Dad. He was kind of pale, but he almost looked flushed compared to Mom's white and drawn face. He had his arm around her. I turned my attention back to Mr. Maclean.

"And then Daniel met Robin," he continued. "They fell in love, and together they were trying to build a better future for themselves. She had started working as a waitress, and he had just been hired as a construction worker. They got an apartment, and were ready to start a family when their dreams came to an end.

Maclean went on to describe how DiGallo had come to Daniel's apartment, trying to collect some money he was owed. The lawyer traced the events of that evening step by step, connecting the dots for the jury. It sounded almost exactly like what Daniel had told me on the sidewalk that day.

"This should be a simple case of self-defense," the lawyer continued. "Unfortunately, because there were no eyewitnesses, the prosecution has pressed for homicide. They want you to believe that Dan found Reggie and Robin together in a compromising situation. That, ladies and gentlemen of the jury, is not true.

"The facts are clear. We have the deaths of three young people. That is very sad, and we want someone to blame. But the only murderer was Reggie DiGallo, and we cannot punish him anymore. As I said, this was a case of self-defense. Mr. Thompson acted as any of you would have done if your home and your loved ones had been threatened. He is innocent of the murder charge."

After finishing his closing remarks, Maclean returned to his table. The judge gave the jury their instructions and they were escorted out of the courtroom. It was already so late, the judge ordered the jury sequestered for the night. We wouldn't hear the verdict until tomorrow.

Chapter Twelve

Daniel stood up and turned around. Mom leaned over the banister and hugged him. He smiled and winked at me over her shoulder as he hugged her back.

In the past few weeks, as the details of the case had come out, Dan had relaxed more and more. His eyes no longer slid over people or looked through them. He could look people in the eye now, and I thought I knew why. Daniel had finally realized that he didn't have to go through this alone.

Mom and Dad had forgiven him a long time ago. Although it had taken me a while, I had forgiven him too. But for our family to be able to move on and try to have a future together, we had to wait until Daniel forgave himself. And he finally had.

By the time we pulled into our driveway, it was already dark. The phone was ringing when we walked into the house. "I'll get it," I said. Mom headed toward her room, already starting to unbutton the sleeves on her nice blouse. Dad was staying with Daniel in Denver.

"Hello?"

"Hi, Shadow."

"Hey, Robin, what's up?"

"Just called to see how things are going."

"Jury's still out, so we don't know anything yet."

"That's good, though, right? The longer they take to make up their minds, the more likely they've found a reasonable doubt?"

"I guess so," I said. "I hope so."

"You doing anything right now?" she asked.

"Actually, Mom decided we should go bowling tonight. Try to get out and move around after sitting all week."

"Sounds good."

"Yeah, but I really suck at bowling." I thought about asking her to join us. Instead I asked, "What are you doing tomorrow?"

"No plans right now."

"Want to go to a movie or something?"

She hesitated. "Won't you need to be with your family? When the verdict comes in, I mean?"

"Yeah, you're right. Maybe next weekend."

"Yeah, that'd be great," she said. I could tell she was smiling.

"Okay. I've got to go. I'll call you tomorrow."

"Okay. Bye."

I hung up just as Mom came back into the kitchen.

"I thought we were going to Olympic Lanes," she said.

"Yeah, just give me a second to go get changed."

"Who was that?" Mom asked.

"Robin."

Her eyebrows went up. "You want to invite her to join us?"

"No," I said. I was looking forward to some time with just my mom.

As I walked down the hall, I noticed that the door to Daniel's room was open. I went in and looked around. For the first time in years, it felt right. It didn't feel abandoned or forced. A pair of shoes was at the foot of the bed, and a sweatshirt was hung casually from the bedpost. There were a few rolled posters in the corner and the partially opened closet door revealed clothes hanging and some even on the floor. The CD case was still sitting on the dresser, with the picture of Daniel and his Robin smiling out of it.

I didn't know what the jury would decide. I didn't know how all our lives were going to play out. But I knew we were going to be okay, because we could depend on each other.

"Hey, Shadow. I'm waiting," Mom called.

"Be right there," I yelled back. Our family had done enough waiting.